Sky Horse

1

MUSTANG MOUNTAIN

Sky Horse

Sharon Siamon

whitecap

Whitecap Books
Third printing, 2003

Edited by Lori Burwash
Proofread by Naomi Pauls
Cover photos by Michael E. Burch (mountains) and Lynn M. Stone (horse)
Cover design by Roberta Batchelor
Interior design by Margaret Lee / Bamboo & Silk Design Inc.

Printed and bound in Canada.

National Library of Canada Cataloguing in Publication Data

Siamon, Sharon.
Sky horse

(Mustang Mountain)
ISBN 1-55285-456-6

I. Title. II. Series.
PS8587.I225S59 2001 jC813'.54 C2001-910986-5
PZ7.S525Sk 2001

The publisher acknowledges the support of the Canada Council and the Cultural Services Branch of the Government of British Columbia in making this publication possible. We acknowledge the financial support of the Government of Canada through the Book Publishing Industry Development Program for our publishing activities.

To Jeff

CONTENTS

Acknowledgements

I wish to thank Dr. Wayne Burwash, an equine practitioner who lives near Calgary, for his advice on equine injuries and recovery.

CHAPTER 1

BEAR COUNTRY

Becky Sandersen looked down at the Mustang Mountain Ranch and let out a howl.

"NOOOO!"

She would never call this place home.

Her cry echoed back from the high walls of the Rocky Mountains all around her. Mustang Mountain rose to the right, the Bighorn Range towered like jagged teeth at her back. Below her, the long low ranch buildings followed the curve of the river.

A big truck and horse trailer had just dropped all the Sandersen family belongings at the ranch and driven away in a cloud of dust. Becky had fled up to the mountain meadow to be alone, even though she knew her parents needed her to help unpack.

She pressed her face to her knees and felt the roughness of her jeans against her cheek. How could they push her around like a bale of hay? How could they dump her on this wilderness ranch where there was no town, no kids her own age, no paved roads, no trucks or cars or ATVs?

Becky didn't cry often. She almost never cried when she was hurt, or sad. The tears that blurred her eyes now were tears of anger and frustration. She lifted her head, swiped the tears out of her eyes and took a long breath. The wind blew strands of her honey-blonde hair across her damp cheeks. She tugged it back impatiently with one hand, dug into the pocket of her jeans with the other and found a ragged tissue.

Enough crying, she told herself, shaking her head. I'm out of tissue, and there's sure nothing else in this miserable meadow to blow my nose on! I'm going to start, right here, right now, to think of a way to get back to a normal life. Somewhere far away from Mustang Mountain.

The wind sighed in the pine trees behind her, as if in sympathy. The same breeze rustled the spiky mountain meadow grass with a whisper of warning. Danger, close by. I shouldn't be up here on my own, Becky suddenly realized.

There were grizzlies in these mountains. The bears were hungry after a cold, wet spring, and there had already been three reported bear attacks. Becky scanned the surrounding mountain meadow, looking for any sign of movement. The grassy slope where she sat stretched up to the pines at higher elevations. Above the pines soared the peaks, so high the snow still glistened in the June sun.

A flicker of movement made Becky drop her eyes to the edge of the meadow. A bear? She sucked in her breath, watching. A reddish-brown animal shambled out of the shadows of the trees. It raised its huge head to sniff the wind.

It was a grizz—a big one. Becky lowered herself carefully onto her stomach, hoping the bear would not catch her scent, would not see her. Her dad had shown her bear droppings near the ranch and places where grizzlies had torn apart dead trees, searching for grubs. Bears were ravenous at this time of year.

Becky lay still, watching the bear. The stiff grass prickled her nose, but she did not dare scratch. Any sign of movement might alert the grizzly that she was there. It scraped at a rock, then ambled a short way down the meadow toward her. Her heart thumped like a drum. She closed her mouth tight, to keep the loud beating sound inside, afraid the bear would hear. It stopped, sniffed the wind once more and lumbered back into the trees.

Becky counted to two hundred, slowly. Nothing moved.

She stood up on shaky legs. Close one! She could not come back here alone, on foot. Grizzly bears were the kings of the mountains, the top of the food chain. They were protected in this wildlife refuge, and, according to her dad, it was people's responsibility to keep out of their way. She would have to stay close to the ranch buildings.

As she ran down the meadow toward the ranch, Becky felt the mountains squeezing in around her. She was even more trapped than she imagined.

The slight figure of Becky's mother, Laurie, came striding to meet her at the ranch gate. She would no doubt have something to say about Becky walking alone in bear country.

But her mother's mind was not on bears. She peered at Becky from under the brim of her hat. "We just got a call on the radio-phone from your Aunt Marion in New York. She wants to send your cousin Alison here to stay with us for the whole summer. Alison insists on bringing a friend, a girl named Meg, and they're coming next week!"

Becky stared at her. Why would her cousin and a friend want to come way out here for the summer? She'd only met Alison once in her life, four years ago, and could hardly remember her. Nevertheless, Becky felt a tingle of excitement. At least she wouldn't be stuck up here in the wilderness by herself.

Her mother shook her head. "I just don't know what to say ..." She gestured around the ranch and then glanced impatiently at Becky. "There's so much to do, getting settled, without looking after two extra kids."

Becky bristled. "We're not kids. Alison and I are thirteen. We don't need looking after."

"I wouldn't be too sure about that! After all, these are city girls. Are you positive you want them tagging along with you all summer long?"

"City girls will be better than nobody!" Becky shot back. "You've made sure I have no other friends," she muttered under her breath. It was so easy to get into fights with her mom. She was always saying things that made Becky mad, treating her like a baby!

Her mother wasn't paying attention. "This is just like my sister Marion. She makes these sudden plans without thinking about anybody but herself. What am I going to do with three girls?"

"You talk about us as if we were some of your horses!" Becky exploded. "Don't worry, we'll stay out of your way. I'll make sure of that."

"All right, I'll let Marion know they can come." Her mother turned away. "And speaking of horses, go and help settle Windy in her stall. She's a bit skittish after being trailered." Windy was her mother's favorite mare.

"Isn't there something else I could do? You know how I hate—"

"Don't be ridiculous," Laurie said crisply. "You've got to stop being so nervous around Windy."

"I'm not nervous. I just don't like her." Becky felt a familiar sinking feeling in the pit of her stomach as she followed her mom to the barns. A skittish Windy could kick you right through a barn wall.

But her mother wasn't listening. Her parents never

listened, Becky thought. They are thrilled about this move to a wilderness ranch. It's their dream come true—to breed mountain horses. But it's not my dream, and I'll die if I have to stay here.

She was looking forward to seeing her cousin Alison and her friend—what was her name? Meg, that was it.

CHAPTER 2

The Horse in the Park

Meg O'Donnell stared up at the electronic departure board at LaGuardia Airport and blinked in disbelief.

"They've cancelled our flight. This can't be happening."

Beside her, Meg's friend Alison Chant gave a tiny bored shrug. "Sure it can. The pilots are on strike, remember?"

Meg felt like screaming. "But they can't have a pilots' strike now," she groaned. "Not when we're finally on our way to the ranch!"

"Don't worry about it," Alison said. "My mother will find a way to get us to Mustang Mountain if she has to fly us there in a private jet."

Meg stared at her. "Don't you want to go to your cousin's ranch?"

Alison shrugged again. "I guess so."

How could Alison stay so calm? Meg wondered. Here they were, ready to board a plane to visit Alison's cousin on a real horse ranch in the western Rockies, and all she could do was shrug! But then Alison was always calm, poised, perfectly groomed. Meg often wondered why Alison had chosen her for a friend. It wasn't that she was actually repulsive, just that she could never get it all together. If her long brown hair looked right, her clothes looked wrong. If she managed, by some miracle, to dress like a normal person, her hair stuck out like a porcupine. Most of the time, she didn't really care, but when she was with Alison, she felt like a Shetland pony beside a thoroughbred. Short, and brown, and shaggy.

Meg suddenly remembered the day, nine months before, when she had met Alison. As usual she, Meg, had been wearing baggy sweats. How was she supposed to know her whole life was about to change?

Meg had been walking her golden retriever, Sam, in an upscale neighborhood they'd never been in before. At the end of a quiet street she saw trees and grass, sloping down to the river.

"Sam, that looks like a park. Maybe you can get off the leash for a run!" Sam pulled toward the park but there seemed to be no way in. The wire mesh fence was high and strong. Too bad, Meg thought. The grass looked so green and inviting beyond the fringe of trees.

As they got closer, Meg saw a special gate for walkers,

shaped like a paper clip. She had just entered the gate, with Sam still panting and pulling, when something large went by the fence an arm's length away.

A horse! Meg caught her breath in that dazzling moment. The smell of him, the sun glancing off his shiny hide. The size and the weight of him! The sound of his hooves on the soft path and the sound of his breath all around her. She was almost close enough to touch him.

Meg plunged forward, catching a glimpse of a large bay horse trotting along a sawdust path, with a girl in neat boots and a white shirt riding expertly, high above her.

Sam was beside himself with excitement. He wriggled himself into a frenzy and caught his leash in the bars of the gate trying to dash after the horse. By the time they burst through the fringe of trees, the horse had disappeared.

Meg was as excited as Sam. Ever since she could remember, she had loved horses. This was the closest she had ever actually been to a real, live horse, and the glorious moment had taken her breath away.

Sam, nose to the sawdust, trotted ahead. Meg followed the riding path down through a tunnel of trees, wondering where it would lead. Twenty minutes later, the path bent sharply to the left and she found herself at the edge of the river. The scene in front of her was so perfect that she gasped with pleasure.

There, in the middle of green lawns, was a big blue barn and a riding ring surrounded by a white fence. The tall bay horse stood near the fence on the far side.

Meg looked for the girl in the white shirt, but she was nowhere to be seen.

A sign on the fence said "Please Keep Back." Meg wound Sam's leash tightly around her fist and climbed onto a low set of bleachers.

"That," she told Sam, "is a horse. Someday, I'm going to have my own horse. So you'd better learn how to act around horses. Let's just sit here quietly and see if the experts are right. Let's see if he'll come to us."

She turned her body so she wasn't staring at the horse and shoved Sam around so he was facing her. "Horses don't like it if you stare at them head-on," Meg explained. "At least, that's what the horse books say."

Sam perched quietly on the bench, making little whining noises in his throat. They sat like that for a long time, with the autumn sun pouring down on them, the warm horse smell rising from the exercise ring. Then, out of the corner of her eye, Meg saw the bay horse moving slowly toward them. "It's working!" she whispered to Sam. "He's coming over to check us out."

"Do you always talk to your dog?"

Meg spun around on the bench to see a tall girl with short dark hair looking at her with raised eyebrows.

"Sometimes," Meg admitted. "When we're alone. I didn't realize you were there."

"I just came back from hacking my horse around the trail." The girl climbed up beside her on the bleachers and Meg realized with a gasp that this was the girl she'd seen on horseback.

"I ... I saw you riding. That beautiful horse—is it yours?" Meg blurted.

"That's Baron." The girl nodded. "He's a ten-year-old Dutch warmblood."

"You have a real dressage horse?" Meg's blue eyes were wide as she gazed at Baron on the other side of the fence.

"Sure," the girl said, as if everyone owned a horse worth thousands of dollars. "You know about horses?"

"Just from books," Meg confessed. "I've never actually been up close to one in my life."

"No?" The girl's question hung in the air. She gave Meg a long look. "You go to St. Mary's School, don't you? I've seen you."

"Y-yes," Meg stammered, suddenly embarrassed. "I'm Meg and this is my dog, Sam."

The girl reached over and gave Sam a quick pat. "I'm Alison Chant," she said. "If you like horses, why don't you come to my next riding lesson on Saturday?"

"Do you mean it? Would they mind?"

"Not if you're with me." Alison jumped gracefully down from the bleachers. "Come and meet the Baron, if you like. He doesn't mind dogs, as long as they behave."

And that had been the beginning. They went over to pat Baron's silky dark nose and talked about horses until Alison's mother appeared in a sleek car to pick her up.

"See you Saturday, at ten," Alison had called over her shoulder as if it were nothing at all. Meg had walked home with Sam, her feet barely touching the ground, thinking only of horses.

*

At first Meg had just watched Alison's dressage lessons. Alison was one of the best riders at Blue Barn Stables. She looked fabulous on Baron, with her neat black helmet and perfectly tailored riding clothes. Meg could have watched for hours as they circled the ring.

Gradually, Meg started helping in the barn, mucking out stalls and carrying food and water. It wasn't long before all the horses in the stable knew her and looked forward to her coming. As she got to know them, it was as if she understood what they were thinking. One horse was playful and bold, another shy and fearful. She learned to brush and curry them, to clean their hooves with a pick and clean their tack with saddle soap. She brought them carrots for treats.

After months of begging, Meg had convinced her mother, a hard-working accountant, to pay for one riding lesson a week. All winter they rode in the indoor ring, and Meg learned the basics. She would never be as good as Alison, but at least she could walk, trot and canter.

Meg knew her mom was right. The girls who owned their own horses were rich like Alison. She lived in a huge house on the river and her older sister went to an expensive school in Italy. Meg lived with her mother and brother in an apartment over her mom's office, on the main street of their suburban town. Still, she couldn't stop dreaming of having a horse of her own. The school horses were fine, but it wasn't the same.

And then had come the sudden invitation to join Alison on her cousin's ranch in the Rocky Mountains for the whole summer. Meg said "Yes!" right away, even though she wasn't sure why Alison had invited her. Who cared? She was going to a ranch where the horses spent their lives on wilderness trails. Every day she would ride, not in a ring, or in a city park, but high in the mountains, where horses used to run free. She was going to horse heaven!

Someone jostled Meg's elbow, and her mind was jerked back to the crowded airport. With this awful pilots' strike, they might never get to Mustang Mountain!

At that moment, Alison's mother came pushing through the milling crowds toward them. "They're adding extra flights to another airline," she panted. "You should be able to board in an hour." She gave the two of them a tight, nervous smile.

"Well, that must be a relief," Alison said, rolling her eyes. Her voice was sour with sarcasm.

Meg stared. If she ever rolled her eyes at her mother like that she'd be scrubbing bathroom tiles with a toothbrush for a week! What was wrong with Alison? Why wasn't she excited that they were on their way to the ranch?

As they hurried to the departure gate, Meg wanted to squeeze Alison's hand. But there had always been something about Alison that said “Don’t touch!” so Meg just put her head down and concentrated on keeping up to her long-legged friend.

CHAPTER 3

The Horse in the Clouds

An hour later, Alison and Meg were side by side in the back of a jet, flying west. Meg had the window seat, Alison the middle, and a large man overfilled the aisle seat.

"This is why Mom and Dad always fly first-class," Alison whispered, pointing to the man's elbow, which had taken possession of the entire armrest between them. "I hate being squished!"

"Never mind," Meg said. "We're on our way."

"I knew we would be." Alison wriggled uncomfortably in her seat. "My mother couldn't wait to get rid of me."

"You don't know that—" Meg started.

"Oh, yes I do! They send me somewhere every summer. This year it's a ranch. Last year it was tennis camp for two whole months. Except that everybody got beaver fever on a canoe trip—even the counselors. We were all sick and throwing up. My parents had to come back from Italy to take me home. Somehow, I knew I wouldn't be going back to Camp Oshawonga!" Alison made a face. "I guess Mother figured Aunt Laurie would keep me out of trouble—and out of her way."

Meg glanced at Alison, but her friend's face was shut up tighter than her brother's bedroom door.

"What's your cousin like?" Meg asked, changing the subject.

Alison reached into her knapsack and pulled out her wallet. "I brought a picture," she said, handing it to Meg. "It was taken four years ago, when we were kids."

Meg studied the picture. A chubby blonde girl sat on a brown horse. A younger Alison, her hair in a ponytail, stood in front of the horse, her hand on its bridle.

"Nice horse," Meg said.

"Just a cow pony." Alison shrugged. "Can you believe it? I was jealous of Becky on that trip because she could ride that old plug. Of course, the next year I got Baron ..." She sighed. "A summer of slopping around on a western saddle is going to ruin my dressage training. And I've been working all year on improving my seat."

The man next to Alison gave her a startled look. Meg stifled a giggle.

"Oh well." Alison stuffed the picture back in her wallet. "Even if we have to ride western and my cousin is a hick, at least I have you. And there might be some good-looking cowboys on the ranch. We'll do our own thing." She raised her eyebrows and smiled at Meg.

Meg tried to smile back. Alison sometimes talked about older guys she'd met on ski trips in that *You know what I mean?* voice. Meg never asked for details. As for the guys their own age—they were totally tongue-tied and drooling in Alison's presence. Meg squirmed uneasily. Boys were another area where Alison seemed more experienced than she was, or even wanted to be. At least, not yet. I guess I know why Alison wants me to come to the ranch, she thought. If there aren't any good-looking guys and Becky's a bore, she's got me—as her insurance policy!

The in-flight movie started and Alison clamped on her headphones, shutting off conversation. By the time the movie was over, the flight attendant was announcing that they would soon be landing in Calgary.

Meg raised the window shade and sunshine flooded into the cabin. The clouds were white and fluffy, and as the airplane descended toward them, Meg saw one in the shape of a running horse, its mane and tail streaming out behind.

"Look at the clouds!" She nudged Alison. "There's one that looks just like a galloping white horse!"

"There's no such thing as a white horse," Alison said in her superior tone. "They're all actually grays, unless they're albinos, and then they have pink skin and blue eyes."

"I know," Meg sighed. "But I can imagine it's a sky horse. If only he were real! If only he were mine!"

Alison glanced at her watch. "We're an hour and a half late. I hope Uncle Dan is still waiting for us at the airport."

CHAPTER 4

A Real Cowboy

The Calgary airport was full of confused and anxious travelers as Meg and Alison stepped off the plane. There was no airline representative to meet them and no sign of Alison's uncle.

"What does your Uncle Dan look like?" Meg asked, hurrying after Alison through the crowded arrivals area.

"He's tall and has black hair and a great big mustache," Alison called over her shoulder. "At least, that's how I remember him."

In the baggage area, Alison found a cart. "You get our suitcases," she told Meg. "I'll look for my uncle."

A few minutes later Meg, pushing a heavily loaded luggage cart, came panting up to Alison. "Any sign of him?"

"Not yet."

"What are we going to do?" Meg was beginning to panic. She had never traveled without an adult and she hated crowds.

"We'll wait. What else *can* we do?" Alison was wearing her bored look, tinged with annoyance. "Quit staring at every man who comes near." She elbowed Meg in the ribs. "They'll think we're trying to pick them up!"

Meg gulped. What a terrible thought. But Alison was right. That guy over there, for instance. Why did he keep glancing at them? He had on a cowboy hat, striped shirt, jeans and cowboy boots with spurs. It wasn't hard to imagine him on the back of a horse, with a rope in his hand. *Stop looking at him!* Meg told herself urgently.

But there was no doubt the cowboy was staring at them. Now he was coming over.

"See what you've done?" Alison hissed. "Ignore him."

"That's not your Uncle Dan?"

"Of course not. Look at those ridiculous clothes. And those pathetic boots. Anyway, he's too young."

Meg grabbed the cart, edged closer to Alison and tried not to look as scared as she felt.

The cowboy took off his hat.

"Excuse me, Miss," he spoke to Meg. "I don't suppose there's any chance that you two girls are headin' for Mustang Mountain Ranch?" He drawled "raanch."

Meg felt limp with relief, but Alison, who had been staring hard in the opposite direction, slowly turned her head. "Who are you here to meet?" Her voice was full of suspicion.

"Well, that's the problem, Miss." The young man gulped. "I forget the names of the girls I'm supposed to meet. I thought Dan would be back by now with the horses. He must have got held up, somehow ..." His voice dribbled off into a mumble of uncertainty.

"Dan who?" Alison wasn't taking any chances. This guy could have got into a conversation with her uncle while he was waiting for her. She'd heard too many stories of girls trusting strangers and never being heard from again. Plus, she didn't like the look of him. That big old felt hat and those grubby worn-down boots!

"Dan Sandersen," the cowboy said hopefully. "The girls I'm supposed to meet are visiting Dan and his wife, Laurie, and their daughter at the ranch."

"Alison," Meg said in a low voice, "this guy must be from the ranch. He knows your uncle's name."

The young cowboy's face cleared. "Alison! That was one of the girl's names."

"Ha! Easy for you to say now." Alison shot a look of disgust at Meg. "Well, all I can say is, I think it's awful that Uncle Dan sent this boy to pick us up, and my aunt's not even here, or my cousin. It's rude, if you ask me!"

At that moment, Meg saw a blonde girl and a tall man with a mustache walk up behind Alison. They both stopped short, listening to her with shocked expressions.

Meg felt a flood of embarrassment. She tugged at her friend's sleeve. "Alison ..."

"Let me finish." Alison twitched away angrily. "We've come all the way across the continent. The least they could do is meet us!"

"Alison, I think they're here ... your uncle and your cousin."

"Where?" Alison whirled around and almost collided with the girl, who took a quick step back.

The two girls stared at each other, turned away, turned back and stared again, like strange horses meeting each other in a pen. If they were horses, Meg thought, Alison was the aristocratic thoroughbred, the other girl a beautiful palomino. Her blonde hair was streaked with sunlight. Her face had a rosy glow from a life spent outdoors.

"Hi, Alison," the girl said. "It's me. Becky."

"Oh," Alison said. "Hello." She tossed her head, not in the least embarrassed.

There was an awkward pause.

Becky turned to Meg with a shy smile. "You must be Meg. Hi."

Meg liked the look of this slender girl. She was dressed in a checked shirt, jeans and boots. She looked easy and comfortable in her clothes, and her brown eyes lit up when she smiled. Meg smiled back.

The tall man's face was flushed. "I'm sorry you were worried we wouldn't show up," he told Alison. "The truth is, darlin', we were here more than an hour ago, and it looked like your flight was canceled. We left Jesse here, in case you showed up. Glad you made it." He patted Alison's shoulder.

Meg saw Alison stiffen at being addressed as "darlin'." Her eyes were still snapping with anger. "Anything could have happened to us," she said. "We were completely on our own."

Dan looked puzzled. "Jesse was here." He shoved his hat down harder on his head. "You're probably going to find a lot of things different out here," he told Alison. "In the meantime, let's get movin'. I've got a truck and two horses in a hot trailer in the parking lot."

He strode away, leaving Alison outraged, and Jesse grinning from ear to ear. "I'll help you with those bags," he said. "Now that you know I'm not some dangerous criminal."

He's laughing at us, Meg thought. He thinks we're spoiled brats.

But if Alison was embarrassed, she didn't show it. "Don't bother. We can manage our own luggage." She jerked the heavy cart forward and insisted on pushing it all the way to the airport doors.

Becky walked beside Meg. "How was your flight?"

"Excellent, once we finally took off." Meg smiled up at the taller girl. "I was so worried we'd never get here!"

"Well, we still have a long way to go," Becky warned. "It's more than an hour by truck, and then we have to ride up to the ranch."

Meg stopped and stared at her. "We're going to ride? Today?"

"Afraid so," Becky said. "We can't drive all the way in to Mustang Mountain. They've got this zone up there where they don't allow any motorized vehicles. I'm sorry."

"I'm not!" Meg cried. She had to keep from dancing. "I love riding."

"Oh ..." A frown puckered Becky's forehead. So this is why Meg wanted to come out here, she thought. She thinks Mustang Mountain is some kind of dude ranch. She glanced at Meg's shining eyes and transfigured face. I might have known—she thinks riding is fun! "It's a long ride, and pretty hard," she told Meg. "You're not going to make it in those shoes."

"We've got riding clothes and boots in our bags," Meg said. She could see that Becky still looked doubtful. She tried to explain. "I'm not as good a rider as Alison, who wins all those prizes in dressage—but I love horses, and I'll try to keep up." She bit her lip. Becky was still frowning. Oh, dry up, Meg, she told herself, she thinks you're hopeless. She stumbled after Becky through the big glass doors, and out into a windy, overcast day.

In the parking lot, Dan's dusty gray pickup was towing a two-horse trailer. "I have to go see about another horse," he told them. "Jesse will make sure you get up to the ranch."

Jesse squinted at the horizon. "Yep, and we'd better

get goin'. We're making a late start, and a storm is building up over the mountains." He slung the luggage into the back of the pickup.

"Not in there!" Alison was horrified. "That's my new Louis Vuitton suitcase."

"Sorry, but there's nowhere else," Becky said. "Come on, we might as well wait in the truck. My dad and Jesse will be talking about horses back there forever."

"Don't you like horses?" Meg blurted.

"Not much." Becky tossed back her shoulder-length hair. "I hoped when you two got here we could talk about something else. Movies, maybe, or music."

This is awful! Meg thought, as she squeezed into the crew cab behind the front seat. Somehow, we've got off on the wrong foot. Alison is still sulking about her suitcase, and Becky doesn't want to talk about horses.

The two of them climbed into the front seat of the pickup, not speaking or looking at each other. Becky squeezed over to give Alison as much room as possible and sighed quietly. Mom was right, she thought. My cousin Alison is a stuck-up city snob, and her friend Meg is horse-crazy—the kind of girl whose idea of a horse is some pampered purebred in a cozy barn. She has no idea what it's like to really work with horses all day, every day.

"Let's get on the road," Jesse cried, swinging into the driver's seat. "You three ready to go?"

CHAPTER 5

The Road to Mustang Mountain

"Don't take any chances." Dan Sandersen leaned into the truck window to speak to Jesse. "If you get to the staging area and the weather looks bad, don't try riding up to the ranch. Bunk in at Benson for the night."

He banged the door shut and a cloud of dust floated into the air. "You look after your cousin and her friend, Becky." He reached through the window to rumple his daughter's hair. "Have a good ride now."

"What does he mean have a good ride? And what's the *staging area?* Are you putting on a play?" Alison sat stiffly, trying to keep her traveling clothes from touching the truck.

Jesse gave a snort of laughter. "That's rich, a play. I guess you're from the big city," he hooted.

"Quit that!" Becky punched his arm. "The staging area is where you pack up the horses for the ride in," she told Alison.

"Horses? These horses?" Alison gestured back at the horse trailer.

"We got them especially for you," Becky said. "You're used to riding English, so Dad found two horses that are used to that style of reining. She looked at her cousin curiously. "What's the matter? I thought you were crazy about riding."

"Of course I am!" Alison said. "But I'm used to riding my *own* horse. He's a champion Dutch warmblood."

"Oh boy," Jesse laughed, "I'd like to see that fancy riding horse on the trail to the ranch. He'd break a leg in the first half hour."

Alison looked down her nose at Jesse. "I suppose that would make you laugh. But trust me, I'd never bring Baron to this backwoods."

As they left the airport and rolled along the highway, Meg wished Alison would stop acting so superior. In another hour the waiting and delays would be over. They were going to ride—today! They were heading up into the mountains to a remote wilderness ranch. Alison, she begged silently, don't ruin this for me!

She stared out the window at the enormous space stretching away to the west. The foothills unfolded like pages of a book in front of them, each one higher than the last.

Meg squirmed around to gaze at the horse trailer

bouncing behind the truck. What would the two horses look like? Would one of them be white like her sky horse, with a flowing mane and tail?

*

Jesse drove fast, even towing the horse trailer, and cornered the pickup like a pro. Half an hour later they turned off the highway and bounced along a gravel road, sending up a huge plume of dust behind them.

"Is it always this dusty?" Alison choked.

"Nope. Wait twenty-four hours and this road will be a sea of mud." Jesse grinned. "There's going to be a gully-washer of a storm." He pointed west, where large banks of clouds rose over the foothills, blotting out the mountain peaks. "Rain, hail, hey! If you're lucky, it might even snow!"

"Snow? At the end of June?" Alison gasped. "You've *got* to be kidding!"

"Snow any time at all," Jesse nodded. "June, July, August—any time."

"Is he kidding?" Alison asked Becky.

Becky shook her head. "Don't mind him. Cowboys like to tease."

Half an hour later, the road left the rolling hills. With the truck in low gear, they twisted up around hairpin turns. "We're climbing Corkscrew Pass," Jesse told them. "We go down the other side and out on the flats, and then we're at the staging area."

"Thanks for the guided tour," Alison said sarcastically. "Shouldn't you drive a little slower around these corners?"

"Don't waste your breath tellin' me how to drive," Jesse suggested. "Save it for riding—you're gonna need it." He swung the wheel in a wide turn, throwing Alison against the armrest.

Meg wished Alison would shut up. Jesse must have driven over this pass a hundred times. If only they could see through the clouds and mist—there must be high mountain peaks all around them.

"We'll most likely hit the rain when we get to the top of the pass," Jesse said. "Your city clothes are going to get pretty wet." He threw the truck into low gear and they climbed higher. A few minutes later the rain began, spattering the windshield with big drops.

"Shouldn't we go back?" Alison insisted. "Uncle Dan said we shouldn't try to get to the ranch if the weather got too bad."

"There's nowhere to turn this rig around till we get over the pass." Jesse gave Alison a lopsided mocking grin. "Don't tell me you're afraid of a little rain ..."

At that moment, Becky screamed. "Jesse, watch out!"

Standing in the middle of the road, at the crest of Corkscrew Pass, was a huge bull elk. Its antlers were as wide as the truck.

"Hold on!" Jesse shouted. He cranked the wheel sharply left.

The truck slithered and slid on the wet road. Cursing loudly, Jesse fought with the wheel. Behind them, the horse trailer swung wildly.

There was a screech and a thump, and all of them were thrown violently forward.

Alison found herself pressed against the window, eyeball to eyeball with a startled elk. The huge animal shook its great head and stalked off with dignity, only slightly dazed.

After the screech and the cursing and the thump, the cab of the pickup was suddenly very quiet.

"Is everybody all right?" Jesse gasped at last. "Is the trailer still on the road?"

"I'm okay," Becky murmured in a shocked voice.

"If you'd been paying attention—" Alison started.

"Never mind that." Jesse winced, trying to turn his body. "Can anybody see the horse trailer?"

Shaking badly, Meg managed to wiggle around and look out the rear window. The trailer was tipped at an angle, its back end resting against the low earth bank at the side of the road. It had been wrenched loose from the truck.

"I think it's okay," she said. "A little crooked."

"Thank God." Jesse took a deep breath. "I was afraid it would go over the edge when we jackknifed. Look, kids, we have to get the horses out of there. If another car comes over the crest, it could crash into the trailer and send it off the cliff."

Meg felt his worry for the horses and liked him for it. Alison was wrong—Jesse wasn't just a dumb cowboy. She could see that he was in pain. He was clutching his left wrist, and a thin stream of blood trickled down his forehead.

Becky reached under the seat for a first-aid kit. She unwrapped a gauze pad and pressed it on Jesse's forehead to stop the bleeding. Her heart was thumping madly.

"My head's okay, but I think I might have broke my wrist." Jesse winced as he tried the door handle. "We have to get those horses out. Alison, go around and open my door."

"Why me?" Alison asked. "It's raining!"

"Because you're sittin' next to the door," Jesse said with a twisted grin. "And if you think the rain is bad, get ready for worse. Here comes the snow."

They gaped through the window. Jesse was right. Big clumps of snow were starting to splat against the windshield.

Becky took charge. "Alison, open that door and get out—it's not going to kill you to get wet. This truck is right in the middle of the road. We've got to move it." She turned to Jesse, who was holding his injured left arm close to his body. "Can you drive?"

"Don't think so ... ," he mumbled.

"Then I'll have to," Becky said. She took a deep breath.

“You can’t drive!” Alison snorted.

“I’ve never driven on a real road, in rain and snow before,” Becky said. “But I’ve driven on ranch roads.” She gave Alison a sharp poke. “C’mon. You two get out and check the horses. I’m going to try to get the truck off the road.”

Alison grumbled about getting out into the wet snow. “This is so ridiculous,” she sniffed. “What kind of a place has snow in the middle of summer!”

As they climbed from the truck, the snow hit Meg’s face like cold wet kisses, so gentle that it didn’t seem dangerous. But the snow was colder than rain. It clung to their hair and clothes, soaking them to the skin. This morning we were at home, she thought. Home, where it was summer, warm and dry.

“It’s freezing out here!” Alison said. “And my stuff is getting wet.”

The luggage in the back of the pickup was blanketed with a mixture of dust, rain and wet snow.

“Ugh!” Alison groaned as she and Meg hauled their muddy bags out of the back of the pickup and ran across the road to the trailer. “Look at my new Louis Vuitton! My mother is going to be furious!”

Meg was speechless. How could Alison worry about her suitcase at a time like this?

She wrenched at the trailer door. Inside, the two horses were still safely held in their partitions, but the sudden stop had upset them. They stamped their feet and rolled their eyes in fear. One was a paint with one blue eye, the other a chestnut with a blaze down its nose.

"It's okay," Meg soothed as she slid the suitcases into the empty space at the front and climbed in after them. She patted the nose of the nervous chestnut and spoke softly to it. "It's all right. You're a good boy."

"What are you doing in there?" Alison stood shivering and stamping in the falling snow, her dark head already capped with white sticky flakes.

"I'm trying to quiet the horses," Meg said. "Then I'm going to put on my riding boots and all the warm things I can find in my suitcase."

"In the trailer?" Alison wrinkled her nose. "It smells."

Meg wished Alison would stop acting like an idiot. As if it mattered that the horse trailer smelled! "It's not that bad," she said. "Come on, you're getting soaked."

"I can't believe this is happening to me." Alison climbed into the trailer and took the sweater Meg held out to her. She pulled it over her head and fluffed up her short dark curls. "I suppose I'll have to wear my jean jacket and a hat, too. It's going to totally wreck my hair!" She lifted a black Stetson out of her carefully packed suitcase and put it on. "How does it look?"

Meg was busy getting into her jeans and riding boots. "Fine," she muttered. The only hat she had was a battered straw thing that made her look like a dumpy donkey. As if it mattered! "How are they doing out there?" she panted, pulling on a waterproof shell and jamming the straw hat on her head.

Alison hopped on one foot over to the trailer's small window, struggling to get her other sleek black boot on at the same time. "My cousin and that loser? Well, she managed to get the truck started. Oh no! Look at this!"

Meg dashed to the window. Out on the wet road, the pickup lurched forward like a frightened horse. It made a couple of wild jerks across the gravel and smashed into a large boulder.

"I told you," Alison said in disgust. "Becky can't drive."

CHAPTER 6

In the Saddle

"Well, that does it." Jesse hugged his broken wrist and grimaced with pain. "We aren't goin' anywhere in this truck."

They stood in the road, surveying the damage. The front end of the pickup was crumpled against the rock, the wheel bent at a crazy angle.

"I'm sorry," Becky moaned. "The road is so slippery —I tried to steer." Her hands were still trembling from the shock of losing control of the truck.

"Not your fault," Jesse mumbled. "Question is ... what are we gonna do?" They stared at each other. Becky knew as well as Jesse what a fix they were in, with the snow coming down and the truck smashed up.

"Can't we just wait until help comes along?" Alison said.

"We could wait a long time. Nobody's going to be driving over this pass in a freak snowstorm." Jesse shook his head.

"Can you ride?" Becky asked. She was worried about Jesse. He looked very thin and cold standing in the falling snow. Besides the pain, he seemed groggy from the bump on his head.

Jesse nodded. "Sure. I'd have to be dead before I couldn't ride."

"There are four of us," Alison broke in, "and only two horses."

"I can ride behind Jesse," Becky said. "You and Meg can double up on the other horse. If we can ride down to the staging area, we can call for help."

"Might be the best," Jesse agreed. "And it might be handy if you knew the horses' names. The paint's name is Hank, and the chestnut is Mike."

"Hank and Mike?" Alison sneered. "What hilarious names! Did you ever see such ugly animals? Their feet are like dinner plates."

"You'll be glad for those big feet before this ride is over." Jesse grimaced.

"Let's go," Becky said. "Jesse, you get back in the truck while we saddle the horses."

This isn't exactly the adventure I dreamed of, Meg thought as they unloaded the horses and hoisted the heavy saddles onto their backs. This is cold and wet and dangerous.

"This saddle is so big and clumsy!" Alison sniffed.

"Good thing, since one of you has to hold onto the back of it," Becky snapped. "Hey, here's a lucky break! Dad tied rain gear on the back of the saddles."

She untied the two big yellow slickers and handed one to each girl.

"You wear them." Alison looked doubtfully at the long heavy coats, split up the back for riding. "Meg and I have our own rain gear." She patted her small black knapsack.

Meg wished Alison wouldn't speak for her in that superior tone. She'd love to wear one of the slickers—her own skimpy jacket wasn't much protection. But it was not worth risking Alison's scorn to say anything.

"Whatever ..." Becky slung the coats over her arm. "What else have you got in there that might be useful?" She reached for Alison's pack.

"Nothing!" Alison grabbed it. "Just my personal stuff," she insisted. "I'm taking it with me."

Becky gave her a look, but said nothing.

"I've got some chocolate cookies from the plane," Meg said, opening her own small pack, "and a flashlight, and riding gloves, and a notebook."

Becky gave her a grateful look. Meg was "horsey" and quiet, but she was focused. "Good. I'll leave a note in the truck in case someone comes along." She ripped a page from Meg's notebook and started scribbling. "Bring the food and flashlight—Jesse probably has matches."

"Why do we need all this stuff?" Alison said.

"Because we don't know what's going to happen!" Becky opened the truck door, shoved her note on the dash and slammed the door shut. "With luck we'll get down to the staging area and call for help there, and it will stop snowing and we can get Jesse back to the doctor."

Meg marveled at Becky's ability to take charge. She's just our age, Meg thought, but she knows what she's doing. If only Alison would stop complaining and let her do it!

"We never should have been out here without your father," Alison said huffily. "It was all his fault, sending us off with this dumb cowboy!"

"That *dumb cowboy* just saved your life twice—by not hitting an elk and by not sliding off a road and down a cliff!" Becky glared at her. "So maybe you'd better not call him names."

Becky's eyes had some of Alison's snap, Meg thought. Looking at them, nose to nose, you could see they were cousins. They stood staring at each other, backs straight, heads held high.

Finally Alison turned with a shrug. "All right, he's a hero! The man of my dreams." She walked over to the paint horse. Hank stood quietly in the road, blinking against the clumps of snow falling in his eyes. "And you're the horse of my dreams," Alison said, climbing onto the saddle. "I just can't wait for this ride!"

Becky ignored her. "Can you hold Mike's head?" she asked Meg. "He's a bit twitchy and I want him to stand quiet while I help Jesse into the saddle. He can't do anything with his left hand."

Meg felt honored to be asked to help. "Good boy," she soothed, and Mike bobbed his head as if he understood.

"We'll lead," Becky said, swinging herself up behind Jesse. She peered down at Meg from under her wide-brimmed hat. "Tell me something. Is my cousin always like this?"

"No!" Meg said quickly. "Not always."

"That's a relief." Becky shook her head. "I wondered how you two ever got to be friends."

Are we friends? Meg asked herself. I was so flattered that Alison wanted to hang out with me that I never realized how different we are—until now. And I *never* saw her like this!

CHAPTER 7

Corkscrew Pass

The road down the other side of Corkscrew Pass was slippery and steep. Meg and Alison leaned back to help Hank balance. The snow was so thick now that Mike was just a swaying shadow ahead of them.

Meg found it hard to stay on Hank's back. She gripped the back of the saddle and tried to relax, but every so often Hank tripped on a stone and she nearly slid off sideways. If only Alison would quit fussing with Hank's reins and hauling up on his head, the poor horse would go more smoothly. This was not dressage.

As the four riders wound their way down the road, a roaring filled the quiet valley. They could hear the river at the bottom long before they saw it, tearing along between flooded banks. The road disappeared at the edge of the water.

"The bridge is out!" they heard Becky shout above the rushing water. She had dismounted from Mike and walked to the edge of the river. "We'll never get across!" She turned back to Alison and Meg with a worried frown.

Alison looked disgusted. "Where's this staging area you were talking about? I thought you said it was at the bottom of the hill."

"It's on the other side of the river, not too much farther on." Becky pointed across the angry torrent.

Meg was fascinated by the furious rush and roar of the river. It looked like a wild animal, tearing at the banks. "What happened to the bridge?" she asked.

"It washed away. It happens sometimes, when we get an early-summer storm," Jesse said, shaking his head. "It must have been snowing and raining in the peaks all night. We're sure havin' more than our share of bad luck."

"Bad *luck?* I don't think so!" Alison said scornfully. "What are we going to do now?"

"There's another bridge farther upriver." Jesse pointed off the road to the left. "It's higher—it might still be holding."

"Should we check it out?" Becky asked doubtfully.

She needed Jesse to help her make this decision, but she wasn't sure he was thinking clearly. Jesse was white with pain. The ride down the hill must have joggled his wrist with every step of the horse.

"I don't think we've got a lot of choice," Jesse said. "It's a bit too cold to swim the horses across."

He's all right, Becky thought. He can still make a joke. No way the horses would survive in that torrent!

"Are you suggesting that we leave the road and go riding off through the wilderness in this snowstorm?" Alison's high voice sounded almost hysterical.

"Alison," Meg protested, "come on. They know what they're doing."

"You think so?" Alison screeched. "I don't. I think this is crazy! Let's go back up to the truck and call for help."

"There's no phone in the truck," Becky told her, climbing back on Mike behind Jesse.

"Then we should ride back to the nearest house," Alison insisted. "At least we'll be on a road, not on some back-country trail!"

"There's no house anywhere near," Becky said wearily, as if she were explaining to a little kid, "and no phone. The closest one is at the staging area. We need to get there."

Alison glared at her cousin, but she hauled hard on Hank's mouth and they followed Mike off the road and onto a narrow trail beside the river.

As they rode, Meg watched every branch, every blade of grass grow thick and fuzzy with clumps of snow. The whole world was turning white. Snow in June! she thought. If only I wasn't so cold, I would think it was beautiful.

In places, the trail wound too close to the flooded river, and Jesse and Alison had to detour off the trail. Here the horses had to step over a tangle of fallen branches and force themselves through willow thickets that slapped at Meg's and Alison's wet jeans. Meg wished she had one of those long riding slickers to protect her legs. It was all so different from riding around and around in an indoor ring!

"Do you know where you're going?" Alison bellowed. "What if this other bridge is washed out, too?"

Meg could see the white cloud of Alison's breath as her question hung in the air. It was a scary possibility, the second bridge being out, but it didn't help to be so negative. She had always seen Alison at school or at the riding stable, where she had everything under control. Out here, it's different, Meg thought. Alison can't get her way, and nothing is under her control.

Hank's breath came in steamy snorts, too. It was getting colder. As they made their slow way down the trail along the river, Meg had the sensation of going deeper and deeper into a still, white world, where the only moving things were the two horses, the only sounds the clunk of their hooves and the jingle of Jesse's spurs. It would be easy to drowse off ...

"There's the bridge!" she heard Becky shout through the snow. "Hurry! It looks like it's about to go any minute!"

CHAPTER 8

DANGEROUS WATER

The river flowed high and swift under the old wooden bridge. It swirled around the beams that held up the bridge and licked at the underside of the planking.

The water smells like high mountains and melted spring snow, Meg thought. It was a wild, exciting smell that woke her from her drowsy state.

"No way I'm going over that!" Alison cried as they rode up to the bridge. "It's suicide!"

"Stay here, then!" Becky called back over her shoulder. "I've got to get help for Jesse."

Meg could tell by the urgency in Becky's voice that she was really frightened. She jumped down from Hank and hurried forward. "What's wrong?"

"He can't keep himself in the saddle without help." Becky's face was tight with worry. "He's so cold, and in so much pain, and I think he keeps losing consciousness because of the bump on his head."

"Oh, go on," Jesse mumbled. "You're exaggerating. I'm all right. Just a little chilly, that's all." But he was slumped over the saddle at a funny angle, and Meg could see that Becky was right. She was holding him on the horse.

"How can I help?" Meg said.

"Lead Mike across the bridge." Becky handed down the reins. "The stupid animal is spooked by the water on the bridge. I can't make him go across."

Meg could see the fear on Becky's face, hear it in her voice. But that was impossible! Becky was an experienced rider. A nervous, skittery horse shouldn't bother a girl who'd been riding all her life. It must be Jesse she was worried about. Meg took the reins Becky handed her, gripped them close to the bridle in her right hand and the ends lightly in her left hand.

"C'mon, Mike," she urged.

Mike didn't move.

"Talk to him some more," Jesse croaked. "Make him think you know what you're doin'."

Meg glanced up at Jesse's white face. He was grinning at her, but it wasn't a teasing grin, she was pretty sure. He was trying to give her confidence.

She took a deep breath. "Come on, boy," she told Mike again, this time in a firmer voice. "It's just an old bridge with a lot of water on it. Nothing to be afraid of." She made kissing noises to Mike and turned him toward her to get him moving. When he took a step forward, she felt like she had won a major battle.

Now for the bridge!

The water curled around the toes of her boots as she started across. The river flowed fast under the old bridge planks. She could feel the boards quiver and shake under her feet, but she forced herself to walk at a slow and steady pace, talking to the horse all the way. "If this bridge collapses while we're on it, we'll all be swept away. Just a little faster. Hurry!"

The chestnut shook his head and blew, as if he understood.

"That's it, Mike, we're almost there—a few more steps ... good boy!"

Meg let out her breath with a rush. They'd made it.

"Good stuff." Jesse tried to smile again as Meg handed up the reins. "I guess not all easterners are marshmallows."

Just then they heard a wail from the other side of the river. "Don't leave me here!"

"Then there's Alison!" Becky's voice was rich with scorn. "It would have been so easy if she'd just come across with us. Hank would have followed Mike, no trouble."

"Come on!" Meg yelled to Alison. "Get off Hank and lead him."

"I'll get my feet wet!" Alison howled.

Meg wiggled her own frozen toes inside her wet boots. "So? Wet feet aren't going to kill you."

"She'd better hurry," Becky said. "The water is pouring down from the mountains. That river is getting deeper every second."

"I'll go help her," Meg said, then called to Alison. "Stay on your horse. I'm coming."

She took another deep breath and plunged into the water on the bridge, which was now ankle deep. This time, she could feel the bridge swaying. This time, she ran.

"Give him a kick," Meg told Alison. "Get Hank moving, and I'll lead him by the reins."

"I hate this," Alison said.

"So do I, but I don't want us to get left on this side of the river by ourselves," Meg insisted. "Come on!"

Alison handed her the reins, grabbed the saddle horn and nudged Hank hard in the sides. Reluctantly he started across the bridge.

"It's moving!" Alison screamed.

Meg could feel the pull of the current on her ankles. If Hank balked in the middle of the bridge, they'd never make it.

"Let's go, Hank," she urged. "Kick him, Alison," she cried. "We're going to run."

The water splashed high as Hank began to trot beside her. Meg was drenched with icy water, but she kept moving. The bridge was groaning under them as the wood beams gave way. With a final burst of speed, they made it to the other side and solid ground.

Just in time! As they turned to look, the bridge gave a last wrenching groan, collapsed completely and vanished into the water. In seconds it was as though there had never been a bridge. The river seemed to gain new energy from its victory and flowed even faster and more dangerously.

Meg shuddered, looking at the black, swirling water. Her breath came in frozen gasps.

"Now we can't get back!" Alison's voice was hoarse with shock. "I thought we were going to drown. I hate this place."

Becky slid off Mike's back. "You might have drowned if it hadn't been for Meg." She gave Meg a grateful smile, and then frowned. "You're soaked to the skin. Alison, have you got any dry clothes in that precious bag of yours?"

Alison's face flushed scarlet with anger. She rummaged in her bag. "Here's some stupid thermal socks, and my nylon shell—"

"A waterproof shell? Great. I'll put it on. Meg, take my slicker. It will help keep your legs warm." She stripped off the long yellow raincoat and handed it to Meg, then pulled the waterproof jacket over her head. "Why aren't you wearing this yourself?" she asked Alison.

"It's new." Alison tossed her head. "I didn't want to wreck it."

"You're amazing," Becky said. "Okay, it's still snowing, and we have a long way to go. Back along the river to the road, then up to the staging area. You ready, Meg?"

Meg yanked off her wet boots, put on the dry socks and shoved her feet back into the wet leather. She wiggled her icy toes again. At least they'd feel dry for a few seconds. She climbed up on Hank behind Alison. The soft flakes of snow had turned to icy sleet.

"Will there be anybody at this staging place?" Alison called as they started off the way they'd come.

"No, but there's a beat-up old trailer with a stove and a phone to call for help. We'll be all right once we get there," Becky shouted.

"If we get there," Alison shouted forward through the stinging snow. "I can't see a thing."

Meg was dying to tell Alison what she thought of her—that she was being a horse's hind end. It wasn't as if Becky and Jesse could do anything about the weather, but Alison acted as if they ordered the snow especially to bug her!

Hank fell in behind Mike as they set off across country. Meg lowered her head so the pellets of frozen snow wouldn't sting her face. Good old Hank—he seemed unbothered by the snow or the rough terrain. As for herself, every muscle in her body ached. She was hungry and cold and tired and scared.

"This is ridiculous," Alison sniffed from in front of her. "As soon as we get to a telephone, I'm calling my mother and telling her to book us the next flight out of here! This is worse than tennis camp."

She's as scared as I am, Meg suddenly realized. She's afraid we might never make it to the phone.

CHAPTER 9

Finding Shelter

"The trail up ahead ... it's most likely flooded by now," Jesse mumbled. He clung to the saddle horn with one hand, trying to stay upright on the swaying horse as they made their way back toward the road.

"Let's hope it isn't." Becky had one arm around Jesse and was holding the reins in the other. She let Mike pick his own way along the snow-covered trail. Jesse was right, she realized with a sinking heart. The flood water was spreading across the low-lying land ahead of them with frightening speed. If they kept going, they could get trapped.

"We could cut across country ..." Jesse struggled to get the words out through lips numb with cold. "It's shorter."

"Do you know the way?" Becky asked anxiously. She hated to leave the river and head into the unknown.

"Just up to the rim of the valley ... along the ridge, cut down when you see the flats ..." Jesse pointed vaguely with his good arm.

"What if it's snowing too hard to see anything?"

"Worth a try ...," Jesse muttered. "Everybody's cold. Can't go on too much longer."

"All right." Becky made a swift decision. "We're going up to higher ground," she called to Alison and Meg.

Without the river to guide them, they seemed to be lost in a world of white swirling snow. They blundered slowly up the ridge, the horses straining with the effort.

On top of the ridge, the wind howled around the horses and riders, and it was harder than ever to see. Worse, Mike was limping. "I've got to stop," Becky told Jesse. "There's something wrong with Mike's left foreleg."

"I know how he feels." Jesse grimaced, holding his damaged wrist.

Becky slid off Mike, hoisted his foot and peered at his hoof.

"What's wrong now?" Alison called from her perch on Hank.

"Luckily, it's just a loose shoe." Becky trudged back through the snow, wiped the snow out of her eyes and looked up at Alison and Meg. "But we really shouldn't ride him until we get it fixed." She took a deep breath. "Besides, we can't see anything while it's snowing this hard. I know we're on top of the ridge, but I have no idea where the staging area is from here."

"We're lost, I knew it," Alison groaned. "What does the brilliant cowboy suggest we do now?"

"How is Jesse?" Meg asked.

"Colder, and still dizzy. I don't think he can make suggestions. I think it's up to the three of us to decide what to do."

"Oh, fine!" Alison said. "This is perfect. I'm freezing to death on this horse, we're lost and—"

"We could find some shelter, get a fire going and wait for the snow to stop." Becky ignored her and spoke to Meg.

Meg nodded. "How long do these storms usually last?"

"A few hours, or a few days." Becky squinted up at her. "The main thing is, I don't want to get any more lost. We could start going in circles ..."

"Then it's better to stop until we can see where we're going," Meg agreed. "What do you think, Alison?"

"Oh, never mind, just get me off this horse and out of this snow! No one listens to what I think anyway!" Alison slid down from Hank's back. "Where is this shelter you're talking about?"

"We passed a small stand of pine and poplar trees in the shelter of a rock cliff a while ago," Becky said. "We could follow our tracks back—"

"Trees!" Alison cried. "I thought you were talking about a building! What good are trees? I'm cold. I'm tired of riding this horse, and I'm wet."

Becky turned on her. "Haven't you ever been cold and tired and wet before?"

"No," Alison said. "I never have. Things like this don't happen in the city."

Becky threw up her hands in disgust. "Not to spoiled, pampered girls like you, anyway!"

The two cousins glared at each other, then Becky stomped off without a word and climbed back on her horse behind Jesse. She would ride Mike as far as their rest stop, just to make sure Jesse didn't fall off. Then she'd try to fix the chestnut's loose shoe. She had no energy to fight with Alison. They would need every scrap of their energy for survival.

Becky's idea of a shelter is no five-star hotel, Meg thought as she slid wearily off Hank's back and surveyed the grove of spindly poplars. The trees looked as weak and beaten by the storm as she felt. The rock wall behind the trees was cold and forbidding, with each crack and crevice outlined in white. Still, it was some protection from the biting wind.

Leading Hank, Meg plunged through the knee-deep snow to the nearest tree and tethered him, making sure his reins were not dragging and his cinch was comfortably loose. He might be here awhile if we wait for the snow to stop, she thought, glancing up into the swirling cloud of flakes.

Becky tied Mike to the next poplar and looked closely at Meg. "You're shivering," she said. "I'm worried that you and Jesse are getting hypothermia."

"I-I'm f-fine." Meg tried to stop her teeth from chattering, but inside her damp sweater and jeans, she had begun to shudder uncontrollably. "Do you really think we can start a f-fire? Everything out here is so w-wet."

"I hope so." Becky tried to smile reassuringly. "Jesse has matches and there's bound to be dry kindling near the bottom of those pines." She pointed to a small cluster of pine trees near the rocky outcropping. "Once we get a fire going strong, we can burn even the damp stuff."

Half an hour later they huddled around a fire made of pine and poplar branches. Becky was right—the dead wood burned even when it was wet. Meg shared her chocolate cookies, and Becky melted snow in a can she found in one of Mike's saddlebags. They sipped hot water from the can.

"I'm imagining this is hot tea," Meg said. "It's warming me right down to my boots."

"Tea!" Alison grumbled. "You've got a vivid imagination!" She waved the can away. "I'm not drinking dirty melted snow!"

Meg passed the can to Jesse. She was worried about him. The blood on his forehead had dried. But his face still looked a peculiar pasty color and he staggered when he walked. She and Becky shared a look of concern as he got up to put more wood on the fire.

At least the fire was warming Jesse up. He had stopped shivering and squatted with his hat shielding his head from the snow. The left sleeve of his slicker hung empty. Becky had managed to tie his injured arm close to his chest with a sling made from his bandanna.

"I don't get it," Alison said suddenly. "Why couldn't we just drive to the ranch like any normal place? I mean, if you hadn't crashed the truck." She looked sideways at Becky.

"There aren't any normal roads, just a wagon track," Becky sighed. "They only drive on it in an emergency." She paused. "And they brought in a truck when they moved us to the ranch."

Meg saw a shadow cross Becky's face when she mentioned moving. Something about that move made her very unhappy.

"Well, if they have a dirt road, I don't see why we couldn't use it," Alison continued. "It must be so inconvenient to ride in all the time."

"They don't use it because the ranch is part of a wildlife refuge," Becky tried to explain. "Bears and other big animals need a lot of territory, so they've tried to make a wilderness corridor through the mountains from Yellowstone to Alaska. Only a few roads and train tracks cross it. They're worried about the animals becoming extinct."

"So why do you live up here if the animals need their great big space?" Alison persisted. "Seems like a dumb idea."

"I agree," Becky poked at the fire with a stick. "If it was up to me, I wouldn't live at Mustang Mountain. But it's not up to me ... none of this is up to me."

Meg looked at her curiously. Becky sounded angry. None of what? Was she upset that she and Alison had come for the summer? If that was true, Alison wasn't making her any happier about it!

"But what are we going to do?" Alison glanced at her watch. "It's already six-thirty. Are we going to stay here all night?"

"It won't get dark until almost ten o'clock," Becky said. She put another dead branch on the fire. "I'd like to stay until we can see where we're going. The snow is bound to stop ..." She glanced at Jesse. His head was drooping, his eyes closing.

Meg scooped another handful of snow into the tin mug and set it down into the coals to steam. She could feel some of the tension inside her loosening with the fire's heat. She had almost stopped shivering. Now that they had a fire, they could wait until the snow stopped. Then it was just a short way to the staging area and a telephone. They'd be all right once they got there. She watched Becky expertly build up the fire and marveled again at the matter-of-fact way she acted, even in a crisis. She was tough.

"I'm going to look for more dry wood." Becky stood up.

"I'll help," Meg said.

"I'll help ..." Alison mimicked Meg's voice. "You're so helpful it's nauseating. Would you like me to help, too, Cousin Becky?"

"No, you just stay here and melt the snow with your red-hot sarcasm," Becky said. Meg could feel another battle coming on between them.

"Go with Becky if you want to ..." Meg got up and stretched. "I'll stay here and keep an eye on the fire."

"I'm sure Cousin Becky prefers you," Alison said shortly. "You two best buddies go on. I don't give a fig what you do."

So that's what's the matter, Meg thought as she plunged after Becky. Alison's jealous because Becky and I are starting to become friends. She feels left out.

Meg jammed her straw hat down over her ears and shivered. She wished Alison would realize they needed to work together, not fight like eight-year-olds in the school yard!

She and Becky slogged through the deepening snow and searched the rocky outcrop for dry branches wedged in the cracks.

"This will keep us going for a while." Becky heaved on the roots of a small dead pine that hadn't found enough soil to survive. She dumped her armload of wood into Meg's arms. "I should check the horses—see what I can do about Mike's loose shoe."

The horses stood patiently, heads down, enduring the snow that was clumping on their eyelashes and manes.

Meg watched Becky lift Mike's foot expertly and wiggle the loose shoe.

"You really know what you're doing," Meg said, admiring Becky's deft touch.

"I don't," Becky grunted. "But I've seen my mom do this hundreds of times. She's a farrier."

"That must be an interesting job," Meg said. "Fitting horseshoes."

"It's a dangerous job." Becky shook her head. "One time my mom was shoeing a horse and it just went berserk, for no reason. It ran into the barn door at full gallop and broke its neck."

"That must have been awful. Poor horse!" Meg had a vivid mental picture.

Becky straightened up and looked at her. "What do you mean, 'poor horse'? My mom could have been killed." She shook her head again. "That's what I don't like about horses. You never know what they're thinking, what they're going to do next."

"Sometimes I feel like I do," Meg said hesitantly. "I can almost feel what they're thinking."

"That's where you're wrong," Becky said. "Don't trust them, that's my advice." She bent over Mike's hoof again. "I need the proper tools to do this ... and they're at the ranch."

"Don't you like Mustang Mountain Ranch?" Meg suddenly asked. "Aren't you happy you moved here?"

Becky didn't answer right away. When she did, her

voice cracked with emotion. "I was supposed to start a new school this year," she said. "But there isn't any school to go to. I have to take correspondence courses! I'm missing everything, and on top of that, I have hours of chores to do every day. I feel like I'm in jail. No friends … nothing but horses!"

Mike suddenly shied and whinnied. "Whoa, boy." Becky quickly stepped back. "See what I mean?" she said. "He's acting weird all of a sudden."

CHAPTER 10

TERROR FROM ABOVE

Mike tossed his head and pulled at the reins tying him to the tree. "Something's spooked him," Becky cried. "And look at Hank."

Hank was pawing the ground and shaking his head. He gave a loud neigh of alarm.

"Maybe they hear something," Meg said. "Horses hear things we can't. Maybe they hear wolves." She felt herself start to shiver again. "I read about how a wolf pack sometimes attacks weakened animals in a storm."

"No." Becky tipped her chin up. "I hear it, too. It isn't wolves. I think it's an airplane."

They stood still, listening, peering up through the white blanket of falling snow.

“Hear that?” Becky grabbed Meg’s arm. “It’s a small plane, flying low.”

The hum of a plane’s engine, muffled by the snow, surrounded them.

“Maybe they’re looking for us!” Alison jumped in the air, waving her arms. “Can they see our fire? Can we signal them?”

“I don’t think they could see anything through this.” Becky shook her head. “It’s too thick. Listen. They’re flying way too low. Maybe they don’t know where they are …”

The noise of the engine was suddenly deafening. They all instinctively ducked—the plane was right on top of them.

“Higher! Get the plane higher!” Becky screamed, as if it would do any good, as if the pilot could hear her.

In the next instant they heard a horrible grinding crash.

“The plane hit the ridge,” Becky gasped, her face white.

“It’s going to explode!” Jesse shouted.

Meg stood by the horses’ heads, trying to quiet them.

The seconds ticked by in silence.

The silence became unbearable. All of them were thinking of the plane, crumpled into the mountainside, somewhere out there in the snow.

Finally Becky swung into action. She untied Mike’s reins, tightened his cinch and mounted the saddle.

“Where are you going?” Alison shouted to her.

“I’m going to look for the plane. There may be people still alive. Come on, Meg—we might need both horses.”

Becky's voice was harsh with shock, but determined.

"Are you out of your tiny mind?" Alison's frightened eyes grew even wider. "We're barely clinging to life here, and you two are riding off to the rescue? What about Mike's loose shoe?"

"These are people's lives we're talking about," Becky shouted at her. "Mike will be all right. Oh, I'm not going to waste time arguing with you!" She wheeled her horse toward the ridge. "I can't believe I'm related to you!"

"What is she talking about?" Alison stumbled through the snow to Meg. "Don't let her just ride off like that!"

"Alison ..." Meg bit hard on her lip. There was no time to tell Alison she was being a selfish, self-centered brat. "I'm going with Becky," she declared. She tightened Hank's cinch and loosened his reins from the poplar tree. Shoving her foot into the stirrup, she climbed into the saddle.

"Meg! You can't! You can't leave me here all alone." Alison clutched at her arm.

Becky called back over her shoulder. "You won't be alone. You'll be looking after Jesse and keeping the fire going. If there are survivors, they'll need that fire."

"Oh no," Jesse croaked. "You're not leavin' her with me. I can take care of the fire. You get goin' now, you're wasting time. And take her with you!"

Alison spluttered with fury. "How dare he—"

"Don't argue!" Becky shouted. "You're staying with Jesse, and that's that. Let's go, Meg."

Meg didn't look back. They rode toward the sound of the crash that still echoed in their ears. Up the ridge to the top, where the wind blew without mercy. The horses put their heads down and plodded steadily through the blinding snow.

Meg strained to see through the thick flakes. "There!" she pointed to the right. "What's that dark patch ahead?"

"I see it." Becky urged Mike forward. "There's something ... it might be a plane."

"Come on, Hank." Meg clucked to her horse, digging in her heels.

As they rode closer, they saw a small cargo plane, bulky and without windows along the side. It slanted into the hill with a broken wing. The snow had already started to bury it.

"Looks like the pilot tried to land," Becky called, her voice awestruck, "but couldn't tell how close they were to the ground."

They got off their horses. Meg felt terrified to go closer. Her imagination painted pictures of torn, bloody bodies strewn around the inside of the plane. There was an eerie silence as they stumbled toward the wreck through the snow, knowing that at any second the plane might explode.

"Hello!" Becky shouted. "Can you hear me? Is anyone there?"

The answer was the last thing they expected to hear. It was the terrified scream of a horse.

CHAPTER 11

Trapped Horse

"There's a horse trapped in that plane!" Meg darted forward.

"Wait!" Becky held her back. "A badly scared horse is nothing to mess with. And there may be people in the plane, still alive. We have to get them out first."

They plunged through the snow to the front of the plane. Through the half-snow-covered window, they could see the slim shape of the pilot, clasped in a safety harness, slumped over the controls.

"It's a woman," Becky gasped. "I think ... I think she's dead."

"No!" Meg brushed the snow away from the cockpit window. "I saw her arm move."

"Oh, Meg, I don't know what to do." Becky turned a frightened face to her. "What if she's hurt really bad? What if she's dying?"

They stood staring at each other in the quiet snow for a second, facing the nightmare truth but still unable to believe it. Finally Meg grabbed Becky's shoulder and shook it. "Come on. If we were that woman, in that plane, wouldn't we want us to try? I mean, even if we can't help her, wouldn't she want us to just hold her hand?"

"You're right." Becky tried to shake off the fear that froze her. "We're wasting time. There could be fumes in there, the horse could strike a spark, kicking the metal. That's all it would take, one spark, and the whole plane could explode. We've got to get her out."

Terrified squeals and thumps rocked the entire fuselage. If they didn't do something soon, the horse would kick it to pieces—if the plane didn't explode first.

"We'll get the pilot out, and then we'll save the horse," Meg said. "Right?"

"If we can." Becky tugged the heavy cockpit door open, and they scrambled into the small space beyond.

A male voice suddenly screamed through the bulkhead behind them. "Is someone there? I think I'm going to have to shoot this horse!"

Becky and Meg gaped at each other. There was someone in the cargo area with the horse!

There were more shattering kicks and squeals from the horse. "Help me out of here! The door's stuck from the inside." The voice sounded young, and hysterical. There were more thuds and thumps. "I'm the horse's groom ... Hurry! Or I'll have to shoot him."

"Please don't shoot the horse," Meg begged. "We're going to get the pilot out, then we'll help you."

"Don't shoot at all!" Becky shouted. "The plane is full of gas fumes from the crash. You'll set off an explosion!"

"All right, but hurry. I'd rather get blown to bits than get my head kicked in—" The young man's squeal sounded as frantic as the horse's.

Meg and Becky glanced at each other. "The pilot first," Becky ordered. They wormed their way forward through the wreckage of the cockpit to the pilot's side.

Meg looked into her face. "She's so young!" she said, her voice breaking.

"She's breathing." Becky was fumbling with the woman's seatbelt.

They unstrapped the limp pilot and laid her back gently on her seat.

"How will we get her out?" Meg felt helpless, looking at that still face.

"Look for a stretcher. There must be emergency supplies somewhere on this plane." Becky was gently removing the pilot's headset.

Meg searched the cockpit and found a neatly rolled-up package with a red cross buckled to one wall.

"Here!" She unrolled the package. "Blankets, a stretcher, bandages, all kinds of stuff." Her hands were shaking.

"We'll need the blankets right now, to cover her," Becky said as they piled the rest of the supplies to one side. "There's not enough room to unroll the stretcher in the cockpit. We'll have to lift her out of the plane."

Meg shook her head. "It's all wrong. In our first-aid class, they taught us never to move anyone in case they have an injury to their spine."

"We'll have to risk it," Becky said. She could smell airplane fuel in the cockpit, a sweet diesel smell that prickled the inside of her nose.

CHAPTER 12

What's That Smell?

Back at the fire, the waiting seemed endless. Jesse squatted close to the heat, his hat down over his eyes, shivering. Alison circled the fire, throwing sticks on the flames, trying to keep out of the smoke.

"Don't just dump the wood on top," Jesse muttered. "Feed the fire, one stick at a time."

"It's a stupid fire anyway," Alison coughed. "Mostly smoke."

"The wood is damp," Jesse grunted. "The way you put it on smothers the flames." He was holding his injured arm tight against his body in its sling.

"I suppose you know all about fires, like you know about everything else," Alison snapped. "Well, I'll have you know I've been to camp three years in a row, and I've got my fire lighter's badge to prove it."

"Hush!" Jesse held up his good hand. "Do you smell that?"

"What? The smoke? Of course I smell it. It's in my nose. I'll never get it out of these clothes—"

"Be quiet," Jesse whispered urgently. "Step away from the smoke. Now do you smell it?"

"Arrgh! Yes! What is that?" Alison wrinkled her nose. A sickening pungent odor filled the clearing.

"A grizz, close!" Jesse reached for a blazing stick and stood up, slowly.

"A grizz? You mean a grizzly bear?" Alison's voice shook. "Where?" She peered into the falling snow.

"Don't scream or make any sudden movements," Jesse warned. "A grizz doesn't see too well. Maybe he just smells the fire and is curious."

"What do we do?" Alison felt a trickle of fear run down her back.

"You should try to get up a tree. Grizzlies can't climb trees." Jesse backed slowly toward the thickest poplar in the grove, motioning Alison to follow.

Alison glanced at Jesse's pale face. He was scared, too, she could tell, but his lips were set in a hard line and his eyes were narrow.

"What about you?" she faltered.

"I'm not going to be climbing any trees with one arm," Jesse said. "I'll try to hold him off with this stick."

Now they saw the bear. The vast swaying shape of a full-grown grizzly lurched out of the curtain of snow. It walked toes in, its head swinging from side to side. A growl came from deep in its throat.

"C'mon," Jesse urged, "jump for that lowest branch!"

The tree branch was way over Alison's head. She made a flying leap for it and wrapped her legs around the trunk. She felt Jesse's good hand grip her leg, not letting her fall while she lunged upward and caught the branch.

With a wild scramble, Alison got herself on the lowest limb of the poplar.

"Higher," Jesse gasped. "You're not high enough!"

"Jesse!" Alison screamed. "Look out!"

The bear rose to its hind legs and gave a full-throated bellow. Its massive jaws gaped open. It was tall, much taller than Jesse, and it was coming straight for him!

Jesse waved the burning branch at the advancing bear and shouted with all his strength, "AAAAAH!"

The shout broke the bear's charge. It tumbled to all fours and shambled toward Jesse, growling and swaying its huge head.

"Jesse," Alison screamed, "come on! I'll help you up." She thrust out her arm from the lowest branch of the tree.

Jesse glanced at her over his shoulder. His face was twisted with pain and fear, but he managed to keep the burning pine branch between him and the bear and somehow stumble backward.

At the last moment he flung the branch at the bear's

face and leaped for the tree, reaching out his good arm to clutch at Alison's hand.

The bear, enraged by the heat, tossed aside the smoking branch as if it were a matchstick and charged straight for Jesse.

Jesse swung his feet up just as the bear's sharp claws raked the tree, leaving deep, ugly gashes in its bark. Jesse hung there, clinging to Alison's arm, unable to use his other hand to grab the tree.

The bear was on two legs again, raking the air just under Jesse's back. Alison could see the fury in its eyes. The bear smell was overpowering.

Alison was sure her shoulder would be torn apart. She had never had anyone's life depending on her. If she let go, Jesse would die. The gaping jaws and curved claws of the grizzly were just below.

She had never known she was so strong. Years of riding, gymnastics classes, dance lessons and swimming had built muscles in her arms she never thought about. Now she could feel them—holding Jesse's wiry body above the deadly claws. She wouldn't let him go! The bear couldn't have him!

"Wrap … your feet around the branch," she panted. "Hold on! Hold on!"

At the last second, Jesse managed to swing his body around the branch. Alison yanked at his slicker until he was up and draped over the branch, out of reach of those long claws.

Alison's shoulder burned and throbbed, but she had won. She had saved Jesse from the bear! This tree, this good old tree would keep them safe.

"He won't ... give up," Jesse moaned. "We have to get ... higher."

Alison didn't know how Jesse managed to cling where he was, let alone how he would be able to climb to a higher branch. His face was beaded with cold sweat, and his lips were blue. His thin body must be tough as steel.

She helped him put his foot on the next branch and boosted him from below.

When they were out of reach of the bear, Jesse laid his forehead against the smooth poplar trunk and gave a low groan of pain.

"We'll never be able to hold on up here," he said.

"Maybe the bear will get sick of waiting and go away," Alison gasped.

"I don't think so." Jesse shook his head. "That bear is mad, and hungry. He'll wait till we fall out of this tree."

CHAPTER 13

Rescue Efforts

As gently as they could, Becky and Meg carried the pilot's limp body out of the plane and laid her on the stretcher on the snow. They wrapped her in blankets and tucked them around her face. She was still unconscious.

"Let's carry her over near the horses, away from the plane." Becky said. Each of them picked up an end of the stretcher and struggled through the snow.

When they were safely out of range of an explosion, they laid the pilot down near where they had tied Hank. He gazed curiously at the strange thing on the ground and shook his head, but seemed to understand he was to stand quietly and wait.

"Now the groom," Becky panted, turning back to the plane.

"I'll go," Meg said. "We shouldn't leave her alone." She looked down at the pilot's still form on the stretcher.

"Hurry then. I want to bring Jesse and Alison up here and get another fire going …"

Meg nodded. She knew Becky was worried about Jesse. Alison would not know what to do in an emergency.

"Just get the groom out, any way you can," Becky told her.

"And the horse, too," Meg insisted.

"Don't take any chances with that horse." Becky shook her head. "If the groom can't manage him, he must be pretty bad."

Meg ran toward the plane. She wasn't leaving that frightened animal trapped in the wreckage, no matter what! She wriggled in through the cockpit door. The door that led to the cargo area was at the rear of the cockpit. Back here, the smell of fumes was stronger. Meg yanked at the heavy door, but it refused to budge.

"Hurry up, can't you?" came the scared voice from inside. "One spark from those hooves of his and we'll all be cosmic dust."

The voice had an English accent.

"I'm trying …," Meg grunted. "The door must have wedged shut in the crash."

"How about the big loading bay on the side?"

Meg climbed down from the cockpit and ran to look.

"It's buried in snow. We'll never get it open!" This was hopeless, Meg thought. They needed shovels and heavy equipment, a doctor and a vet to rescue the crash survivors—not just three thirteen-year-olds and a badly injured cowboy!

"If you can't open the cargo bay, find a crowbar or something to pry this door open," she heard the voice shout. "Hurry, if you can. Silver Bullet is quiet now, but he might start kicking again any minute."

Meg searched the cockpit and found a long metal bar. She shoved the end into the crack in the door and leaned with all her might. "Push!" she shouted to the groom, and with a mighty heave they both managed to open the door enough for him to squeeze through into the shattered cockpit.

"Thanks! Fancy being rescued by a kid like you. Where are your parents? Where's the pilot?"

Meg found herself looking up into the face of a boy in his late teens holding a rifle in his hand. He had very pale skin and blond hair that looked as if it had once been gelled into spikes, but was now plastered to his forehead with sweat and dust. He was wearing a fancy western outfit, and the thought flitted through Meg's mind that Alison would approve of the way *this* cowboy dressed.

"The pilot's hurt," she managed to say. "My friend and I are here alone. At least, there's another girl and a guy down the hill, but he's injured too ..." She looked him up and down. "You weren't hurt in the crash?"

"Naw. I landed in the hay, lucky for me. Just shaken up a bit. So you're the entire rescue team. Well, let's go, then. My name's Henry, by the way." He stuck out his hand. "Yours?"

"Meg. What about the horse?"

Henry shook his head. "He's called Silver Bullet, and that's a good name for him. Ever since I got him untied he's been ricocheting around in there like live ammunition! I'm just lucky to get out alive."

"You said you're a groom," Meg insisted. "Shouldn't you know how to handle a frightened horse?"

Henry sighed. "I *said* I was a groom. That doesn't mean I *am* a groom. A brilliant liar is what I am. Now, can we get out of here?"

Meg stared at him. "You *lied* about being a groom?"

Henry pushed her back toward the cockpit door. "Yes, I'll tell you all about it once we're safely out of this aluminum bomb." He brushed past Meg and leaned out the open door. "Great flying fruit bats! This isn't California." He blinked at the snow in disbelief.

"Okay, you're out," Meg said. "Now tell me what you're doing here."

"Hey, I'm just traveling the world a bit, looking for some fun," Henry said. "I happened to be hanging around the horse show at Spruce Meadows when this rich bloke came by, looking for a groom to fly his horse to California. Now, that's a place I've always wanted to see …"

Henry jumped down from the plane, the rifle still in his hand. "Let's get clear of this heap of tin. It could still blow sky high!"

"You can't just leave the horse in here." Meg didn't budge.

"Oh yes I can! You haven't been shut up with old Silver Bullet for an hour. The horse is demented. A kicking, screaming fiend, he is. I thought my last hour had come. I was ready to shoot him right between the eyes."

"It was your own fault for pretending to be a groom!" Meg said angrily. "The poor horse—he must be scared to death. I'm going in there!" She squeezed back through the door to the cargo bay, leaving Henry gaping behind her.

"You're as crazy as the horse!" she heard him shout. "He'll kill you."

Inside the cargo area, the light was dim. The air was full of dust and the smell of horse sweat and manure. Meg could hear Silver Bullet snorting and pawing the floor. Every sound echoed around the hollow metal bay. The noise must be maddening him.

As her eyes adjusted to the light and she saw him clearly, Meg swallowed hard. There he was—her sky horse come to life!

Silver was almost totally pure white, tall and beautiful, with a fine long head. He stood at the end of the cargo area, head down, exhausted with his struggle. But Meg could see that he was young, maybe just a yearling.

She stood perfectly still, hardly daring to let her

breath out. One wrong move, she knew, and he could erupt into a frenzy of flashing hooves. How was she going to get him safely out of the plane?

Think! she told herself. You have to think like a horse —win his trust and make him want to come with you.

But that might take hours, and there was no time.

Outside the plane, Henry plowed through the wet snow to introduce himself to Becky. "I'm Henry Blake." He held out his hand. "This is a nice mess we've got ourselves into, isn't it?" he said. He knelt by the stretcher and looked into the pilot's face.

"Her name's Julie," Henry told Becky. "Poor girl. She shouted back that there was something wrong with the plane, we'd gone off course and she was going to try to land. That was just before we hit."

"I'm Becky Sandersen. Where's Meg?" Becky looked wonderingly at Henry. He seemed as out of place on this mountain as a visitor from another planet.

"She shut herself in with that maniac of a horse." Henry shook his head. "I wouldn't go back in there for a million pounds!"

"What's the matter with her? We need shelter and fire and food, but she's got to rescue a horse!" Becky threw up her arms.

"I can give you a hand," Henry said.

Becky nodded gratefully. "There's stuff on the plane we can use. Just be careful ... you can smell gas fumes in the cockpit."

"No fires in there, then, right?" Henry tried to grin. "I get the picture. Drag out everything that isn't nailed down. You seem pretty smart for a kid. How old are you?"

"Thirteen," Becky said as they plunged back toward the hulk of the plane. "You?"

"Seventeen," Henry told her. "You mind telling me where we are?"

"Somewhere near the Panther River. The truth is, we're lost, too. We can't find our way in the snow."

"You're on horseback, I see ..." Henry pointed to the two horses. "Where were you headed, if you don't mind me asking."

"I live at the Mustang Mountain Ranch," Becky explained. "There's no road so we have to ride in. I'm here with my cousin and a friend, that's Meg, and Jesse, a ranch hand."

"Jesse is the bloke Meg told me about," Henry nodded, "the one who's got himself hurt." They had reached the plane and wormed their way into the cockpit wreckage. "So where is he now?"

"Down the ridge, with my cousin, Alison," Becky said with a worried frown. "They don't have any horses. I hope everything's okay."

CHAPTER 14

DEEP IN TROUBLE

From their perch in the poplar tree, Jesse and Alison watched the infuriated grizzly bear prowl the clearing, find Alison's pack and rip into it.

Alison hid her face against the tree. "Nooo ... not my bag! I shouldn't have left it."

"All that fuss ... over a few fancy clothes," Jesse grunted.

"It's not just clothes! There's something in there I care about!" Alison flared at him.

Jesse stared at her, but in the next second they were both nearly flung from the tree as the bear charged at the trunk.

Jesse's face went white again. "We're going to be

shaken out of this tree like ripe plums," he moaned. "Man, do I wish I had two good arms."

"Can he knock the tree down?" Alison's voice was shaky.

"Maybe. He'll try." Jesse gulped. He had his good arm wrapped around the tree trunk.

"What'll we do?"

"Hold on ... as long as we can. If I fall, don't you come down and try to help. He'll kill us both." Alison saw a wave of pain cross Jesse's face as the bear hit the tree again with all the force of its concentrated rage.

Alison swallowed hard and clutched Jesse's sleeve. "I won't let you fall!"

"Nothin' ... you can do." Jesse's voice was slurred and slow. "I'm feelin' a bit dizzy ..." He shook his head from side to side, trying to clear it. "The Native people out here say the spirit of the bear is strong."

The bear was attacking the tree, up on its hind legs, its claws deep in the bark, throwing all its weight against the trunk. The top of the tree swayed back and forth like some wild ride at an amusement park.

Alison glanced desperately around. The snow was still falling, not as hard as before, but still so hard she could see only a short distance. To their right was a high ledge of rock, with tumbled boulders on top. With every whip of the tree, they came a little closer to the ledge.

"Jesse!" Alison pointed to the rocks. "Could we try to jump to the ledge on one of these swings?"

"We might make it," Jesse said. "But the bear would just come after us ... grizzlies can climb rocks."

"But it would give us a little time. Maybe we could get away, find the others, something!" Alison saw that Jesse was giving up. He was so cold and in so much pain, or maybe the blow to his head had confused his mind. If she didn't do something soon, he was just going to let himself slide away from her and fall.

Alison clutched his arm. "Come on. Let's give it a try."

Jesse gave her his lopsided grin. "Okay, Al," he said. "Next time he flings us at the rocks, we jump."

The bear lunged at the tree. "One ... two ... three ... GO!" Jesse yelled.

They let themselves fly into space. Alison had the breath knocked out of her as she hit the cold rock face. Her fingers clutched at the ledge and her feet found a foothold.

Jesse was a little higher, lying flat on the ledge itself. At first Alison thought he was knocked out, but he groaned and rolled onto his side.

The bear filled the clearing below with its bellow of rage.

"Come on," Alison urged. "Get up. We have to find a place to hide before it comes after us."

"Can't ... get up ... ," Jesse mumbled.

"Get up!" Alison poked at him. "On your feet. We're getting out of here!" She dragged at Jesse's good arm, kicked at his leg and got him moving.

"You're tough, Al." Jesse shook his head. "Don't know why you bother with me."

"Because I don't want to be left out here by myself, that's why!" Alison pushed him up the rocks from behind. "You're not much use, but you're better than nobody."

But movement was painfully slow—Jesse was at the end of his rope. She couldn't make him go faster.

Alison glanced down at the bear. It had stopped shaking the tree and bellowing, but now it was sniffing the air. It would be after them in seconds, once it got their scent.

Ahead of them was a crack between two boulders. Alison shoved Jesse toward it.

"Come on!" she said again. "We're going in there."

"Too small ..." Jesse shook his head.

"We don't have a choice. Take off your hat."

She took the hat Jesse handed her and flung it over the ledge. It lodged in the rocks halfway down. Alison hoped that would keep the bear busy for a few seconds, just as her pack had. She shut her eyes tight, refusing to think about what was in the bag, now ripped to pieces.

Jesse squeezed his head into the crack, turned his shoulders sideways and squeezed farther in.

"How much space is back there?" Alison panted.

"Not much ..." Jesse was cursing under his breath with the pain in his wrist. It seemed to wake him out of his trance. He wriggled with more vigor through the crack until all but his boots had disappeared.

"Keep going." Alison shoved at his boots. She could hear the bear growling in frustration, tearing at Jesse's hat.

"I'm at the end." Jesse's voice sounded hollow from inside the small cave.

"Then curl up. I've got to get in there, too."

Alison heard more grunts and curses as Jesse tried to change position.

Behind her she could smell the bear—hear its sharp claws scrambling over the rock. It was coming fast.

"Jesse!" Alison screamed. "Help!" She dove head first into the cave, felt something catch at her boot, then Jesse caught her under the arm and, with one last effort, yanked her inside.

"That was close," she panted. "Thanks."

"We're going to wish we'd stayed in that tree," Jesse said in a hopeless whisper.

"W—why?"

"Because now it has us trapped ... we're in the bear's den."

Alison turned and looked at the narrow tunnel she had come through. "You think the bear can squeeze through that?"

"Yep. This is his den all right. Can't you smell it? He'll be after us in a flash."

"Then we have to stop him." Alison felt around in the dim light, forcing herself not to gag at what might be on the den floor. "Here! I've got a big flat rock ... help me wedge it in the tunnel."

Jesse used his good arm and together they managed to force the rock sideways into the opening, shutting out the light. “It might confuse him for a while,” Jesse sighed, “but don’t get your hopes up, Al. That bear will figure out another way to get in.”

CHAPTER 15

SILVER BULLET

"Come on, Silver Bullet," Meg whispered to the tall white horse. "We're in this together." She crouched low in the cargo bay, her body turned so he would not see her as a threat. She kept her hands close to her body—a horse could think outstretched fingers were claws—and her eyes averted. Hunters stared at their prey straight on. She must not appear to be a hunter.

"I'm nothing you need to be afraid of," Meg coaxed in a low voice. "I'm not going to hurt you."

In her mind she tried to see what the horse saw. He had a blind spot right in front of him, so she stayed clear of that. He could detect motion a long way off and pick up sounds and smells no human could sense. Like the smell of fear. She must be as steady and quiet as possible and, above all, not be afraid.

She took a step toward him.

Silver Bullet gave a start and pinned back his ears. His right front hoof began to paw the floor of the cargo bay.

"All right. I'm not coming any closer," Meg promised. "I just want you out of here. I'm going to get someone to help, all right?"

The horse lifted its head and softly whinnied. It was as if he were answering her. Meg's heart went out to him. Even after all he'd been through, he was willing to give her a chance.

She squirmed through the door, back to the cockpit.

"Well, I never thought we'd see you in one piece!" Henry had his arms full of gear. "I didn't hear any kicking and screaming in there. Is he dead?"

"Of course not. But we still have to get him out," Meg said. "He won't come for me."

"Meg, it's just a horse, and we don't have time," Becky urged. I would *never* have the nerve to go in there like Meg had, she thought. But then, Meg doesn't realize how dangerous a horse like that can be!

Henry tipped his head to one side. "Silver Bullet is not exactly 'just a horse,'" he said. "He's a Danish warmblood yearling destined to be a champion show jumper. Do you know what he's worth?"

Becky shook her head. She didn't know and didn't care.

"Round about half a million dollars, that's what."

Henry glanced at the closed door to the cargo bay. "The owner, Mr. Oscar 'Moneybags' Douglas, will be very happy if we save Silver's miserable hide."

"I don't care how valuable he is," Meg said. "He's trapped and he's frightened!"

"What about the pilot? What about Jesse? Have you forgotten about them?" Becky wanted to shake Meg. These horse-crazy people were all the same. If there was a horse to worry about, then never mind human beings!

"Silver could help," Meg argued. "We'll need another horse to ride."

"Ha! Good luck riding Silver!" Henry snorted. "I'd sooner be on the back of a fire-breathing dragon!"

"Becky could ride him," Meg retorted. "She's been riding horses all her life."

"No, I couldn't!" Becky exploded. "Nobody could ride him after what he's been through, and he's probably too young to be saddle broke, anyway. Neither of you have any experience with untrained out-of-control horses. You don't know what you're up against—" She stopped suddenly. They were both staring at her, wondering at her outburst.

"He's much calmer now that Henry left," Meg pleaded. "And when he sees you, he'll know he's in good hands. Please, Becky … just lead him out of the plane."

Becky felt herself being squeezed into a smaller and smaller space, like a bucking bronc in a rodeo chute. "I—can't!" she blurted.

"Why not?" Meg asked. "He'll know he can trust you, that you have lots of experience. Horses can sense that kind of thing."

"You're right. He'll sense that he *can't* trust me." Becky looked down. "He'll sense that ... I'm afraid!" It was as if the words were wrenched out of her.

"What?" Meg exclaimed. "Afraid of horses?"

"When I was four," Becky said in a low voice, "a horse I was riding bucked and threw me off. All I remember is the horse rearing and plunging and its hooves pounding down around my head." She waved her hands helplessly. "I can't lead Silver Bullet out. He'll know I'm scared."

"But Alison said you rode every day!" Meg said.

"Not because I want to," Becky shot back. "On a ranch it's something you *have* to do—not something you *pay* to do."

"Whew!" Henry said. "Well, there goes our half-million-dollar horse."

Poor Becky, Meg thought. No wonder she doesn't like horses. Suddenly a lot of things about Becky made sense. "It's okay," she told Becky. "There must be another way ..." She glanced over at Hank and Mike, tied to the trees. "If he smelled the other horses—he might come out by himself."

"Is Silver loose?" Becky asked doubtfully.

Henry nodded. "How else do you think he was chasing me around? I managed to undo the stall straps before he went completely mad on me."

Becky took a deep breath. "All right, then. We have to shovel the snow away from the door and pry it open. Meg's idea might work." She gave Meg a grateful grin. Now that her fear of horses was out in the open, it didn't seem like such a terrible thing. It was as if she could almost see it shrinking, melting like the snow they trampled underfoot.

Henry found a piece of the broken wing, and they used it as a shovel. With all three of them shoveling snow away and prying on the cargo bay door, they managed to open it wide.

"There," Becky panted, rubbing her hands together to warm them, "it's up to Silver now."

CHAPTER 16

IN THE CAVE

Alison trembled in the darkness. Her head touched the top of the cave. The grizzly's den was really just a hollow space under three large boulders. The stench was overwhelming, choking. Above her, where the boulders came together, was a slit covered in snow. "I can't hear the bear," she whispered. "Maybe it's gone."

"Gone to find another way in ..." Alison felt something soft pressed into her hand. It was Jesse's bandanna. "Tie it around your leg if it's bleeding," he mumbled. "Did he get you bad?"

"No ..." Alison swallowed a sob. Jesse's sympathy was harder to take than anything else. "My boot saved me."

"Good thing," Jesse said grimly. "I've seen a grizz tear all the flesh off a man's calf with one swipe."

Alison shuddered. Beside her, she could feel Jesse shivering. He was so cold and he had taken off his sling so she could tie his bandanna around her leg. She took off her jean jacket and wrapped it clumsily around him. Her hand touched his cheek. It was like ice.

"Th—thanks," Jesse stuttered through chattering teeth. "You're ... a brave kid, Al. I'm sorry your bag ... got chewed up out there."

For some reason, Alison liked it when he called her Al. She'd never had a nickname before. She'd always been Alison Chant.

"It's okay," she muttered. "It was just that this model horse I had, Star, was in the bag. I've had him since I was five."

"Meant a lot to you, eh?" Jesse was still shivering violently. Alison could feel the cold creeping through her own sweater.

"My dad gave him to me." Alison paused. "It wasn't his idea to ship me out here for the summer—that was my mom!"

"You didn't want ... to come. No wonder, then."

"What do you mean, no wonder?"

"No wonder ... you've been actin' like a filly that doesn't want to be fenced in. Fighting everything—mad clean through."

"I'm not—" Alison started. "Well, maybe I am mad.

I hate it when my mom ships me off like a package. She doesn't want me." Alison swallowed and cleared her throat. She put her head down, pretending to tie Jesse's bandanna around her leg.

"Hey, Al, it's okay." Jesse wrapped his good arm around her shoulder and gave her a shivery squeeze. "You're a brave kid, like I said. Whatever comes, you can handle it. How about the way we jumped out of that tree, eh?"

His arm didn't make her feel any warmer, but Alison felt something inside her melt. She wanted to cry, but she held back. "You don't think we're going to get out of here, do you?" she asked.

"Not unless a miracle happens," Jesse said. "That bear's out there, trying to get in. If he does, make all the noise you can and hit at his nose. It's a bear's tender spot."

Alison felt around for a sharp rock.

CHAPTER 17

PLEASE, COME OUT!

Back up on the ridge, Meg kept one eye on the plane while they got a fire blazing and rigged a rough shelter of tarpaulins over Julie, the pilot. A couple of times, Silver whinnied and Hank and Mike answered. Meg could picture the young horse trying to work up the courage to poke his nose out the door. If only he would come out on his own.

Henry and Becky lifted Julie's stretcher onto a bed made of pine boughs facing the fire. She moaned and her eyelids flickered, but she didn't respond when they called her name.

"I wish this snow would stop," Becky sighed. "Someone must be out looking for us by now."

"We might have to spend the night," Henry said. "We'll need lots of firewood." He found an ax in the emergency tool kit and attacked the nearby trees, chopping off branches to burn.

"I'm going down the ridge for Jesse and Alison before it gets dark," Becky told Meg, swinging herself into Hank's saddle.

"I'll come, too," Henry said, dumping his load of green branches near the fire. "You might need some help." He strode toward Mike. "Can I ride the other nag?"

"That nag, as you call him, is a great mountain horse," Meg told him loyally. "But he's got a loose shoe. Becky could fix it, but she needs tools."

"There's a hammer in that tool kit." Henry gestured to the pile of gear from the plane. "Any use?"

Becky got off Hank. "Very useful." She dug in the tool kit for the hammer. "We can really use the extra horse and some help to bring Jesse back." She lifted Mike's forefoot across her thigh and tapped the horseshoe nail back into place. "That should do for now."

"Hey, where'd you learn to do that?" Henry asked, astonished.

"My mother's a farrier," Becky said. "She shoes horses for a living."

"You say you're scared of horses, and then you just lift a hoof, casual like, and pound a nail into it?" Henry said. "How do you know he isn't going to kick you to kingdom come? I'd never have the nerve!"

Becky shrugged. "You lift his foot, so he can't kick." The fear inside her seemed to shrink a little smaller. "Do you mind staying alone with Julie while we ride down to get the others?" she asked Meg. She felt suddenly glad Henry was coming with her. He still looked and acted like a space alien, but she liked his smile.

"No," Meg said. "I want to be here in case Silver tries to come out. I've got some oats and water for him." She had been melting snow in a pan from the plane's survival kit.

Henry flung himself into Mike's saddle. It was obvious he wasn't much of a rider. "Hand me that gun, will you, Meg?" he asked, pointing to the rifle.

"You won't need that," Meg said.

"Never know. This is the wilderness," Henry insisted. "I'll feel safer if I have it."

Meg got the gun. If he shoots like he rides, she thought, he'd be safer without it.

She watched Becky and Henry until they were shadows in the falling snow, then went back to tending the fire and watching Julie. The young pilot didn't move or make a sound, and the quiet closed around Meg like dread.

Silver Bullet gave a lonesome whinny from the wrecked plane. He knew the other horses had gone.

"But I'm still here," Meg whispered. "Please come out."

CHAPTER 18

UNDER THE BOULDER

Alison could feel Jesse's head heavy on her shoulder. He had fallen asleep.

"Wake up," she nudged him. "Tell me a joke. Tell me what you used to do when you were a kid." Jesse was suffering from a hit on the head and hypothermia. Her best chance of keeping him alive was to keep him awake.

Jesse sat up and bumped his head on the rock. "Ouch! Where's my hat?"

"The grizzly ate it," Alison said. "I'm sorry, but it gave us a little time to get away."

"But it was my favorite hat," Jesse moaned. "I got it at a rodeo down in Wyoming. It had this braided band made of horsehair. Three hundred and sixty-five strands of horsehair in that band. One for every day …" His voice trailed off.

"Wake up!" Alison insisted. "Did you ride in the rodeo?"

"Little roping competition, nothing special," Jesse mumbled. "I'm a pretty good rider, you know. What am I gonna do without my hat?"

"If we ever get out of here, I promise I'll buy you a new hat," Alison said. "But you have to stay awake."

"Sure …," Jesse said, but she could tell he was dozing off again.

"I ride in competitions, too." Alison nudged him again. "Dressage."

"Is that where they wear the funny hats and coats?"

"They're not!" Alison flared, and then grinned in the dark. "You're teasing, aren't you?"

"Do you like it?" Jesse asked. "All that dressage stuff?"

"Sort of … but I get really, really nervous," she admitted. "My mom was a junior national champion. I'm always trying to live up to … what she expects."

"Must be tough," Jesse mumbled. "I lost my mom and pop when I was twelve. Been on my own for seven years."

Sitting there in the cold, damp cave, it was as if they could tell each other anything.

"I'm sorry," Alison said, patting Jesse's cold hand.

Where were Becky and Meg? Why were they taking so long? Maybe there had been a terrible fire and they were hurt or dead. Maybe she and Jesse were alone out here, with the bear waiting outside.

She looked up at the snow-covered slit of light above her head. Was it her imagination, or was the light fading? Could it be getting dark?

She put her face up to the crack between the rocks to shout for help.

There was a sudden snarl. The bear was on top of the rocks—right above them! Alison felt a shower of wet snow on her face. She shrank back in terror. The bear's claws had reached through the slit, almost slicing her face.

Alison screamed. "Jesse, look out!" She flung herself backward as far as the small cave would allow, knocking Jesse out of reach of the raking claws.

The long claws curved around a bulge in the rock. The bear grunted and heaved.

"Jesse! It's moving! The bear's moving the rock," Alison whispered hoarsely.

"He wants food ..." Jesse's voice was slow and resigned. "He'll tear the cave apart to get us, like he tears apart a stump to get a bug. It's no use ... bear's spirit too strong." His head slumped forward.

Alison grabbed her sharp rock and hammered at the bear's paw. She hated that bear. It wouldn't stop? Well, neither would she. The bear's spirit was strong? So was hers! It wanted to eat? She wanted to live. She was too young to die—and so was Jesse. It wasn't getting either of them.

The grizzly let out a roar of surprise, but did not stop

rocking the boulder back and forth. They could hear it grate on the other rocks.

"It's coming loose," Jesse mumbled. "No use, Al!"

"Hit it, Jesse, hit its paw as hard as you can." Alison thrust a stone into Jesse's good hand. "Don't give up!"

*

Becky and Henry rode into the clearing. It had taken a long time to find it in the snow. "The fire's out." Becky jumped from Hank in dismay. "Where have they gone?"

"I thought you said they had no horses." Henry slipped awkwardly from Mike's saddle.

"They don't. Maybe they set off on foot to find us." Becky scanned the clearing. Snow had covered most of the tracks around the fire.

"There's something here ..." Henry bent over scattered shreds of cloth in the snow.

Becky hurried over to see. She picked up a scrap of black nylon fabric, a dented and crushed yellow CD player. Her face got white and tense.

"This was Alison's bag ... ," she said slowly.

"Looks like *it* exploded." Henry held up another black scrap. "It's been torn to shreds. Look, there's more bits of it over here, by this tree."

Becky dropped the ruined CD player and ran to the tree. She picked up Alison's leather riding glove, or what was left of it. Her fingers traced the deep fresh scars in the poplar bark.

"Grizzly!" she gasped, turning a horrified face up to Henry. "Look at this tree! It's almost been torn apart, too. Alison and Jesse must have tried to climb it."

"So where are they?" Henry looked around. "I don't see any sign ..."

Becky had her head down, fighting for breath. Her stomach was heaving. "Last week," she murmured, "there was a grizzly attack. The bear killed a fisherman. Then it dragged him away. They found his body buried in a stream bank, partly eaten."

"Great heaven!" Henry's voice shook. "You don't think it's killed them and dragged them off!"

"Some grizzlies aren't scared of people anymore." Becky swallowed hard. "Sometimes they attack." She gave one last look around the clearing and trudged slowly back to Hank. "We should look for them—ride in circles around this clearing."

"You don't think we'll find them alive, do you?"

Becky brushed a damp strand of hair out of her eyes. She was trying not to cry. "No."

Henry untied the gun from his saddle. "Good thing I brought this—" he started to say.

"But, Henry ...," Becky began.

At that moment they heard shouting from the top of the rock cliff. They looked up to see a huge boulder teetering on the edge and, above it, a monstrous bear.

"Look out!" Becky shouted.

The boulder came crashing down the cliff straight at them.

At the same moment, there was the crack of a gunshot —then Henry and Becky dove head first in different directions, out of the path of the oncoming boulder.

The boulder thundered between them and crashed into the poplar tree, snapping it like a matchstick.

Dazed, Becky sat up in the snow. From the top of the cliff, someone was screaming.

CHAPTER 19

A Lucky Shot

"GET OFF HIM! Get off him. I won't let you hurt him!" Alison pounded and kicked at the bear.

"Al." She heard a muffled groan. "Stop. Get me … out."

Becky and Henry came scrambling up the cliff. Together, the three of them managed to drag Jesse out from under the bear.

Henry stared at the grizzly's massive body in shock. "Good shot, if I do say so myself. I've never shot anything bigger than a rabbit before."

Becky and Alison clung to each other for a moment, tears streaming down their faces. "I thought we were going to die," Alison sobbed. "It pulled the rock away and came for Jesse, and I thought he—"

"He's not in very good shape." Henry knelt by Jesse's side. "I think he's passed out."

"Oh, poor Jesse." Alison fell to her knees. "He was so brave. He climbed the tree, and then we jumped to the cliff, and then the bear was clawing at the cave and we pounded at it ..." She put her head down on Jesse's chest. "It's all right now ... you'll be all right."

Alison's face was smeared with mud and tears. "Come on," Becky said, wiping the tears from her own eyes. "We've got to get out of here. That bear will wake up." She pointed to a yellow dart buried in the bear's flank.

"What do you mean?" Henry said. "The bear's dead. I shot it."

"You shot it—with a tranquilizer gun," Becky told him. "Come on, let's get Jesse back to the shelter."

They half carried and half slid Jesse down the cliff and roped him to Hank's saddle. He had recovered consciousness but was too weak to hold on with only one hand.

Alison climbed up behind him. She looked back at the clearing—at the split poplar tree, the scraps of her knapsack. It was a tough fight, she thought, but *we won!* And Jesse was right—I was brave. I can be brave when it matters—when someone else matters. She put both arms around Jesse, took up the reins, and they rode out of the clearing.

*

Up at the crash site, Julie opened her eyes and looked straight at Meg. "The radio," she said clearly. "Flares. Let them know where we are."

"Where are the flares?" Meg bent over her. But Julie had closed her eyes and drifted off again.

Should I go and look for them? Meg wondered. If they had flares, they could set them off after dark. Her watch already said eight-thirty. Even with the long June twilight, night would soon fall.

This day seemed endless. This morning she had been packing to leave for the airport. Meg thought of her cozy bedroom, with clean sheets and warm blankets ... Her head drooped, then snapped up with alarm. Where were the others? What was taking them so long?

She ducked out of the shelter to peer down the ridge. The snow was letting up but there was no sign of Becky, Henry or the others. Meg had a moment of panic. What if she was really alone up here? What if they never came back? "If Becky was here, she'd know what to do," Meg whispered to herself.

A nervous whinny from the plane made her spin around. There was movement at the door of the plane—a long white nose and two ears, pricked inquisitively forward, appeared in the opening.

"Silver Bullet," Meg breathed. She wasn't alone! Her beautiful sky horse was here. He was curious, or hungry, or just tired of being by himself—horses are social animals and he was just a yearling, used to being with others.

Meg ducked back inside the shelter and grabbed the pail of oats. She took off her long yellow slicker and hat. Nothing about her must spook Silver. She took a few slow, careful paces toward the plane and held out her hand, keeping her body turned partly away from the doorway and Silver Bullet.

"Come on, Silver. I have something special for you," she called softly. "Nothing's going to hurt you, I promise."

Silver pawed at the metal aircraft body and, when it made a noise, jerked back with an alarmed snort.

Meg was in an agony of frustration. If she could just help him down that step to the ground! He would be all right once he was off the plane. She kept moving forward, slowly but steadily.

"Some great tasty oats in here," she told Silver. "The best you've ever had."

The young horse gave another nervous whinny and pawed at the metal doorsill. Meg was within reach of him now. She knew it was dangerous to go closer. Silver could panic and rear. She set the bucket down and squatted not far away, off to one side.

She could tell Silver was sizing her up and she kept talking. "Dogs like me," she told him, "and most cats, and even some wild things, like raccoons and squirrels. People say I have a natural talent with animals. I wish you'd just trust me."

Silver nickered a small whinny and tossed his head. He was asking for her help.

Meg couldn't stop herself. She slowly stood up and climbed into the plane's cargo bay to stand beside Silver's head. She held her hand flat so he could take oats from her palm, and as he munched them, she reached for the dangling lead rope.

"All right," she breathed, talking gently to Silver. "This is the hard part. The metal at the edge of the bay is all crumpled and bent from when the plane crashed. It's noisy and shiny, but you just walk over it, and then take one short jump to the ground. Trust me, now. It's only a few steps."

Silver Bullet's whole body was on alert. She could see his skin twitch and feel his fear. Meg remembered Jesse's advice when she led Mike across the flooded bridge. Act confident! She took big breaths and forced herself to be calm.

"Come on, here we go." Holding his head close to her body, Meg inched across the rough metal, step by step. Once, Silver caught a hoof on a piece of the crumpled fuselage. He whinnied in alarm.

"We're almost out. Jump!" Meg took a quick leap off the cargo bay into the snow and felt Silver take flight beside her. They'd done it. He was safe on the ground.

"Good boy," she whispered. "Here's your oats, just like I promised."

She watched with joy and pride as he buried his nose

in the bucket. How beautiful he was. Someday, he'd be a champion show jumper, she was sure.

And then, as Silver moved away, Meg's hand flew to her mouth to stifle a cry.

The young horse was lame in the right foreleg.

Somehow, in the crash or all his thrashing around, he had injured himself. Meg knew from her reading that a leg injury could be serious trouble for show jumpers and racehorses. Sometimes, they were even put down!

The limp was slight, but real. Silver took a few more steps and whinnied uncertainly.

An answering whinny came from below. Meg took her eyes off Silver and tried to see through the falling snow. Two horses were climbing slowly up the ridge. On the front of the first, Jesse was slumped over Hank's neck. Alison was bent protectively over him, urging Hank on.

Then came Henry and Becky on Mike. Meg ran forward to meet them. She stopped in astonishment at the sight of Alison's face. "What happened?" Alison was glowing with excitement and her face was streaked with dirt.

"It doesn't matter," Alison said. "Help us get Jesse into the shelter."

"They were attacked by a grizzly." Becky got off Mike and held the reins while Henry flopped to the ground.

"Attacked!" Meg gasped. "By a bear?"

"And I shot him, just in the nick of time." Henry's cheeks were flushed with triumph. "It was a good thing I had that gun."

"The bear isn't dead," Becky whispered to Meg. "It was a tranquilizer gun."

Henry was still grinning proudly. It didn't matter. The tranquilizer dart had saved Alison's and Jesse's lives.

They all helped carry Jesse into the shelter, wrap him in blankets and lay him beside Julie.

"Oh," Jesse said drowsily, stretching out at full length. "That feels so warm … and good." He gazed up at Alison. "Al … you should get your leg cleaned up and bandaged."

"I'm all right." Alison finished tucking the blankets around him.

Meg was standing opposite her. She blinked at the expression on Alison's face. She was dirty, and smelly, and bloody from the battle with the bear, but she was more real and relaxed than Meg had ever seen her. And, for once, Alison didn't seem to care about how she looked. She was obviously thinking about Jesse.

At that moment, Jesse rolled over and looked into Julie's face. "Julie!" he tried to sit up. "What—how—what's wrong with her?"

Alison tried to get him to settle down. "She was flying the plane that crashed," Meg said. "She's unconscious."

"She opened her eyes once while you were gone," Meg said quickly, "and said we should use the radio and set off flares."

"She's talking—that's great news," Becky sighed. "I hope she'll be all right."

"She's got to be!" Jesse's face was twisted with alarm.

"I—I know Julie. She's *got* to be all right."

Alison felt her heart drop. Jesse was obviously crazy about Julie. Alison moved wearily away and let Meg take over. She suddenly realized how exhausted she was.

Becky draped a blanket around her shoulders and handed her a cup of hot tea. "Here. Let me help bandage your leg. What have you got tied around it?"

"Jesse lent this to me," Alison said, unwrapping the grubby bandanna as if it were a designer scarf. "We ..." She glanced over at Jesse, who was still lying with his eyes riveted on Julie's face. "Don't throw it away," she said with a catch in her voice. "I'd like to keep it."

Henry stuck his head in the shelter a few moments later. "Becky, love, can you give me a hand? It's getting dark. We should take a look at the radio and search for those flares while there's still enough light in the cockpit."

Since shooting the bear, Henry has decided he's in charge, Becky thought with a smile.

They trudged back to the plane together.

"I wish Julie could tell us how this thing worked." Henry banged on the radio. "It seems completely dead. This whole plane gives me the creeps. I can't believe we survived the crash!" His rosy cheeks were suddenly pale again.

Becky knew what he meant. The cockpit was cold

and still reeked of aircraft fuel. "Chances are the radio was set to the right frequency before the crash," she murmured. "If we can just get some power, we might be able to send out a mayday signal."

"How do you know about all this stuff?" Henry said. "You're the most amazing kid."

"We have radiophones at the ranch," Becky explained. "We're out of reach of normal cell phone networks."

"Lord, what an exciting life you lead!" Henry had recovered his enthusiasm. "Real adventure!"

"Do you think so?" Becky grinned at him.

"Are you joking? Blizzards, plane crashes, fighting grizzlies, riding up here in the mountains—what would *you* call it?"

"Being a ranch kid is boring, most of the time, I guess."

"Boring! No, Becky Sandersen, you've got it wrong. Other people's lives are boring. *Yours* is exciting!" Henry grinned and ran his fingers through his hair till it stuck up in tufts.

Becky laughed. He was very good-looking when he smiled like that. "I guess it is. Look, I think I've found the flares." She pulled out a red box from a compartment in the cockpit.

"Good work," Henry said. "Now all we need is an auxiliary battery. If I can hook it up to the radio, it might work. And then let's get everything outside. I don't like all these fumes."

*

They set off the flares from the top of the ridge as darkness fell. Henry fired each one from a short stubby red gun. They arced into the sky, turning the falling snow into a red glow of lovely, individual flakes.

"Let's hope you have a lucky shot like the one that got the bear," Meg prayed. "Let's hope somebody sees them."

"Who says it was a lucky shot!" Henry looked hurt. "It was brilliant shooting, that's what it was."

Meg and Becky exchanged knowing glances.

"Save a few of those flares," said Becky, "in case we have to stay another night."

"I hope we don't," Alison sighed, watching the red glow fade. "Jesse needs a doctor."

"And Julie!" Becky reminded her.

"Of course," Alison sighed. "Julie, too."

Poor Alison, Becky thought. She's in love with Jesse, but he likes Julie.

She glanced over at Meg, whose eyes followed Silver's every move. She had managed to tie him with the other horses, but she was the only one who could go near him. And poor Meg, too, Becky thought. She is crazy about a horse that belongs to somebody else.

"What are you thinking about, Becky Sandersen?" Henry flopped down beside her. "You look like you're a million light-years away."

Becky felt herself flush, feeling Henry so close beside

her. She was glad he couldn't see her face clearly in the fading light. "I'm thinking that I hope my friends decide to stay, if we get back to Mustang Mountain," she sighed. "After all we've been through, I wouldn't blame them if they wanted to leave!"

CHAPTER 20

Dawn Light

In the middle of the night, the weather suddenly changed. A warm wind blew over the mountains, clearing the sky. The horses felt the difference. Meg heard them moving restlessly, nickering to each other in the dark.

Henry finally found a battery and got the radio working.

"Mayday! Mayday! Mayday!" Becky yelled into the speaker. "This is Becky Sandersen, calling anyone out there, over."

There was no response except the radio's crackling and spitting. "They might be able to hear us," Becky said wearily.

She repeated her message over and over, telling anyone who might be listening where they were approximately and that the pilot urgently needed medical help.

They took turns feeding the fire. Jesse and Julie were deep asleep. They tried to wake Jesse every hour, and once or twice Julie regained consciousness and even sipped a little water.

Henry settled down on a rough bed of pine boughs and fell asleep in the middle of a sentence. Becky tossed a blanket over him, trying not to look like she cared.

"I'm too stiff and sore to sleep," Alison sighed. "My leg hurts, and my shoulder feels like it's on fire." She shrugged it in a painful circle.

"Me too," Meg murmured. "Every time I shut my eyes, I feel like I'm still on a horse, hurtling down a steep hill."

"And me," Becky sighed. "I keep thinking ... what should I be doing? What have I forgotten to do?"

"You haven't forgotten anything," Meg said. "It's totally amazing the way you looked after everything." She gave Becky a quick hug.

"I left Alison and Jesse alone with a bear," Becky muttered, "and I was afraid to rescue Henry ... afraid of poor Silver."

"Anyone would be scared after being thrown from a horse and almost trampled to death," Meg said.

"What did I miss?" Alison broke in. "Who got trampled? When?"

"When I was a little kid," Becky said. "My horse bucked me off and then tried to stomp on me." She paused and tucked her hair behind her ears. "My parents made me get right back on a horse, so I wouldn't be scared of riding ..."

"But not the same horse!" Alison's eyes were wide with disbelief.

"Of course not! But I guess I never got over being afraid of what any horse I'm riding might do next."

"Wow!" Alison breathed. "Meg's right. Anybody would be scared after that."

"I guess so ...," Becky said slowly. "It's funny how much better I felt after I just ... admitted I was afraid out loud. I guess that's part of the reason I've never liked horses. It was partly getting bucked off, and partly my mom and dad just *expecting* me to love riding as much as they do."

"I know what you mean," Alison sighed. "My mom expects me to be a champion like she was. And I don't even fight her. I just keep on trying to please her. After today, I'm going to stop worrying so much about what people think of me!"

Becky laughed. "My mom always says she came out west to get away from your mom—her big sister. She says no matter what she did, Aunt Marion could do it better!"

"Really?" Alison turned an eager face to Becky. The firelight lit up her dark eyes. "I guess Mom has always had to be the best."

"Talk to my mom about it." Becky nodded. "That's why she started riding western and stopped doing dressage."

Meg looked at them enviously. "You two are lucky. I wish I had a cousin to talk things over with."

Becky grabbed Meg's hand. "After what we've been through today, I think we should make you an honorary cousin. What do you say, Alison?"

"We'll drink to it," Alison said. She got up stiffly and opened the emergency ration box. "Let's have a celebration." She grinned. "There's stuff in here we haven't touched yet."

She pulled the box over to the fire.

"Hot chocolate mix!" Meg cried. "I love hot chocolate, and we've got boiling water."

"Power bars with nuts and chocolate chips!" Alison was pawing through the box. "Dried apricots and ... freeze-dried spaghetti?"

"A feast!" Becky rubbed her hands together in glee. "Should we wake up Henry?" She glanced over to where he was stretched out beside Jesse, sound asleep and snoring loudly.

"Let him sleep," Alison said. "The mighty hunter had a long day!"

They sat up talking and drinking mug after mug of hot chocolate as the sky slowly grew lighter. The warm wind melted the snow until it was just white patches against the dark ground.

"It's almost five-thirty in the morning, and I still don't feel sleepy," Becky sighed. "I'm never going to forget this night."

"I'm never going to forget a lot of things ..." Alison was quiet for a moment, then chuckled. "Like the look on your face after you drove that truck into the rock!"

"And I'll never forget the look on yours when you first got in the truck." Becky grinned. "You looked sooo disgusted!"

"Or how about the look on Meg's face when Dad and I appeared at the airport, and you were screaming about how rude we'd been!" Becky giggled.

"Sorry about that." Alison blushed.

"It doesn't matter." Becky shrugged. "It all seems so long ago."

"Look!" Meg pointed. The sky above the dark wall of mountain peaks in front of them was turning pink and pale blue. As they watched, a finger of purest orange light touched the highest peak, turning it to gold.

"I've never, ever seen anything so beautiful," Meg breathed. "We couldn't see any of this yesterday but it was all around us."

"That's Mustang Mountain," Becky said. "See how it looks like a horse's head, with his mane flying back in the wind?" Meg felt Becky reach for her hand, and she in turn reached for Alison's. The golden light crept down the face of the mountain, reached the river valley and turned the winding ribbon of water to shimmering silver.

Then the moment was gone, and they were just three cold, shivering girls on the side of a mountain.

Becky stood up, shielding her eyes to see better. "I

think I see horses, crossing the river, down in the valley."

Meg and Alison looked where she pointed. A string of horses, some with riders, some with packs, were crossing the river at a wide bend.

"It's my dad!" Becky shouted. "They're coming to get us! Here! We're up here!" She waved and shouted and they all joined her, knowing they were too far away to be heard or seen.

"Smoke!" Becky cried. "We need lots of smoke. They'll see that!"

They heaped wet branches on the fire and fanned the smoke with a blanket.

"It's working!" Alison jumped up and down with joy. "They're heading this way."

They sat down again to wait, panting with the exertion.

Meg watched the horses slowly making their way up the mountain and suddenly realized what it meant.

"What's the matter, Meg?" Becky asked. "You look so sad."

"Oh," Meg said. "I was just thinking about Silver. His owner is going to take him away, maybe worse."

Becky's face grew serious. "Dad will be able to tell us about Silver's injury," she said. "He trains horses, and he knows about that stuff. Don't give up." She found herself thinking about Henry. He'd be leaving, too. Maybe they all would. It would be so lonely. Perhaps if she tried to prepare them for Mustang Mountain a bit …

She put her arm through Alison's. "I have to warn

you about the ranch. It's not exactly luxurious. I mean ... it's probably not exactly what you're expecting."

"Don't worry." Alison smiled dreamily. She glanced over at the shelter, where Jesse's sleeping form was just a mound under the blankets. "I have a feeling I'm really going to like Mustang Mountain."

At that moment, the sound of a loud engine made them all turn to the west. A helicopter hovered over the ridge, then touched down near the wrecked plane. Its whirring blades whipped up a wind, flapping the tarpaulins and bringing Henry staggering out of the shelter.

The three girls ran to meet the paramedic who jumped from the helicopter.

"We got your message last night," he shouted. "How's the pilot?"

"Still semiconscious," Becky shouted back. "And we have a guy with a broken wrist."

"I'll take a look." The paramedic stooped low into the shelter.

Within minutes, Julie and Jesse were ready to board the helicopter. Julie was strapped to a stretcher board, with an oxygen mask over her face as a precaution.

Jesse came over to say good-bye.

He was beaming. "The medic says Julie will be fine," he told them. His thin face grew serious. "He said you two saved her life by getting her out of the plane and keeping her warm. I won't forget it."

He turned to Alison. "You'll be at the ranch when I

get back, won't you? I've never had a chance to thank you for saving *my* life."

"I didn't," Alison said. "That was Henry, with his gun."

"We'd never have been alive when he got there if it hadn't been for you, Al." Jesse grinned at her. "Besides, you promised me a new hat, remember?"

Alison pretended to be squinting at the sun. "We'll be at the ranch," she said. "Go get your wrist fixed up."

An hour later the pack string rode into their camp. Dan Sandersen and two other men from the ranch were leading three packhorses, one with large wooden paniers on both sides, wrapped in canvas.

Dan embraced Becky in a bear hug. "You look fine for a girl who spent the night in a mountain storm." He smiled down at her. "I've never seen snow like that in June!"

He scanned their camp and nodded his approval. "Good fire," he said, "and a shelter. And the horses secured. I'm proud of you."

"Did you bring the horses some feed?" Becky asked. "They're almost exhausted."

Dan Sandersen's eyebrows went up. "Naturally I brought feed," he said. "And bacon and eggs and pancake mix for the rest of you. Let's get that fire built up."

Soon the fire blazed and everyone squatted in front of

it, wearing warm, dry clothes and eating hot food cooked in a blackened pan.

"This girl of yours is a wonder." Henry shook his head as he wolfed down a huge breakfast of scrambled eggs and pancakes. "She took care of all of us."

Becky blushed. Something about Henry's smile turned her insides to melted butter. She had introduced Henry to her dad as Silver Bullet's groom, leaving out the details.

"Your boss, Mr. Oscar Douglas, has been on the radio-phone every half hour since he heard about the plane crash," Dan said. "He's making arrangements to ride up here as soon as he can. How's his young horse?"

"He hurt his leg, Dad," Becky said. "We want you to take a look at him."

The pancake Meg was chewing suddenly stuck to the roof of her mouth. This was the moment she'd been dreading.

But Silver wouldn't let Dan get near enough to examine his leg. He reared and plunged and squealed in fear when anyone approached him.

"I don't know," Dan said slowly. "We'll have to take it easy on our way into the ranch, let him just follow the pack string on his own and hope that limp doesn't get any worse."

CHAPTER 21

Mustang Mountain At Last

The string of riders rode over the last hill and looked down at Mustang Mountain Ranch.

The sun had real warmth and the snow had melted away like icing sugar on a hot cake, leaving everything lush and green.

Becky rode up beside Meg. "Well," she said, "there it is. What do you think of the place?"

"It's perfect," Meg sighed. "Just like I imagined it."

"Seeing it through your eyes makes it look good even to me." Becky smiled. It was true. Meg's enthusiasm was catching.

Her mother was waiting anxiously for them at the ranch house. She enveloped Becky in a hug, then held out her hands to Alison and Meg. "I didn't realize you three were missing until Search and Rescue called," she said. "I thought you were with your father—he thought you must have stayed in Benson because of the storm. I'm so glad you're all right! What happened?"

"We'll tell you about it later," Becky yawned. Suddenly all three of them realized they could hardly stand up for weariness. Later, they couldn't remember having warm baths and eating toasted cheese sandwiches. They only remembered falling into bed and sleeping as though a mountain had fallen on them.

The next morning, the girls found themselves the center of attention in the ranch kitchen. Henry had been spreading stories all around the ranch.

"Did you really clobber a bear with your bare hands?" the cook asked Alison, as he set a huge platter of scrambled eggs and bacon in front of her.

"Well, I—" Alison started.

"And you rescued that million-dollar horse out of a wrecked plane?" One of the ranch hands shook Meg's hand. "They're making you girls from the east tough these days."

"How about this Becky Sandersen?" A second cowboy poured himself coffee from a tall blue pot on the stove. "The way she rescued the pilot, and got the radio working, and shoed a horse in her spare time."

"Leave the girls alone and let them eat." Becky's mom breezed into the kitchen through the swinging doors. "I've got something for you, Meg."

She handed Meg a silver horseshoe. "This is Mike's loose shoe. I thought you might like to have it for good luck. Just make sure you hang it so the ends point up, or all the luck will spill out."

"Thanks, I will." Meg rubbed the smooth, worn shoe.

"And there's something for you too, Alison." Laurie put her hand in her pocket. "Jesse is back from the hospital with good news about Julie. He stopped to pick up the horse trailer at the top of Corkscrew Pass this morning, and found this inside. He thought it might belong to you." She held out a scruffy brown model horse.

"Star!" Alison leaped out of her seat. She hugged the battered toy horse to her. "My mascot ..." she explained to the startled faces around the table. "I never go anywhere without him. I thought he was in my bag that the bear ripped up." She gulped. "I thought I'd never see him again ... and Jesse found him for me!"

"He must have fallen out when you were changing your clothes in the trailer, right after the accident," Meg said. She exchanged glances with Becky. So that's why Alison was so worried about her bag.

"I was embarrassed to be carrying him around." Alison smoothed Star's tangled mane. "I didn't want you guys to see him."

"He's like a lucky charm," Becky said. "What's wrong with that?"

"Nothing," Alison laughed. "Star, you *are* a lucky charm. I'm so glad you didn't get eaten by a bear!"

"I've been on the radiophone to Marion and your mother, Meg," Laurie went on. "They want to know if you want to come home after all this."

Alison looked down at Star. Jesse must have remembered how much Star meant to her. He really did care.

"No," she said slowly. "I think I'd like to stay. How about you, Meg?"

"You don't even have to ask." Meg was beaming.

"Good." Laurie's smile faded. "I'm afraid there's some bad news, too. Silver's owner has arrived. He wants to talk to you when you're finished breakfast."

None of them could eat another bite. They ran outside, where a short, plump man wearing an enormous cowboy hat and a navy blue blazer leaned on a fence, watching Silver limp around a small pen.

"Good morning. I'm Oscar Douglas," he introduced himself. "That's my yearling. I had to helicopter up here to see him last night. No roads—unbelievable!"

He turned to Becky. "It's your mother's opinion that the colt has a tendon injury, caused by the sudden stress of the crash. On top of that, he was traumatized by the accident and won't let me or his groom go near him. We tried getting him in a trailer and he nearly attacked young Henry."

"But Henry isn't—" Meg started to protest.

"Never mind that. I've got to put this horse down." Mr. Douglas shook his head. "Mrs. Sandersen seemed to think I should tell you three."

"You can't!" Meg choked. Silver looked so alive standing in the morning sun, so perfect except for that limp. He lifted his head, whinnied and trotted around the pen.

Meg could hardly see for the tears blinding her eyes. "Oh, Silver," she murmured. "Mr. Douglas, you can't destroy this horse. Please, just give us a few days to see if we can get him better."

"I'm an exceedingly busy man," Mr. Douglas said. "I don't have a few days, and it would take longer than that anyway. Besides, it's bad business." He took off his hat and scratched his bald head. "This horse is no good to me, you see. With a tendon injury and psychological trauma from the crash, he'll never be a great jumper." Mr. Douglas shook his head firmly. "He can't even be trained or trailered in this condition!"

"What does my mom say?" Becky asked.

"She thinks there's a chance the tendon might heal," Mr. Douglas said. "She thinks lots of rest, fresh mountain air and hydrotherapy might do the trick."

"What's hydrotherapy?" Meg whispered to Becky.

"Treatment with water, like walking or standing in a cold mountain stream," Becky said out loud.

"These things are all expensive in California," Mr. Douglas said. "Too time-consuming, with no guarantee of success. I can't risk it."

Meg felt a huge bubble of hope rising inside.

"I can!" she almost shouted. "I can walk him in the river," she cried. "I can do the therapy every day. Silver

Bullet is not afraid of me! Please, Mr. Douglas—give him one more chance."

"I'm not sentimental about horses," Mr. Douglas insisted. "I don't keep them because they're nice to look at—I'm a businessman. It's a lot of work rehabilitating a horse."

"There are three of us," Becky said. "We'll help Meg."

"Silver will be as good as new by the end of the summer," Alison promised.

Mr. Douglas took off his hat and mopped his forehead with a polka-dotted handkerchief. "It goes against all my rules of good business. Ordinarily ..."

"Please!" Meg begged. "Silver's not just an ordinary horse. He's special. You weren't there when he jumped out of the plane on his own. You don't know how much spirit this horse has. He's brave, and strong, and for horses like this you *have* to bend the rules."

"Hmm." Mr. Douglas seemed to be considering the idea. "There may be something in what you say. All right. I'll be back in this part of the world in late August. I'll give you and Silver Bullet until then. Do what you can, but don't break your heart on him." He was looking at Meg as he said, "Spirit is one thing, but tendons are another!" He jammed the hat back on his head and strode away.

Meg felt limp with relief. "We won!"

"Now the hard work starts," Becky reminded her. "We have two months to get Silver Bullet back in shape."

Meg watched Silver circling the pen. Her sky horse. For the whole summer he would be hers. And wherever he went in his future career, winning competitions in California or Copenhagen, there would be a bit of the mountains in him. We can do it! Meg thought, lifting her eyes to the peak of Mustang Mountain, high above the ranch.

At the end of the day, Becky took them riding up to the mountain meadow overlooking the ranch where she had seen the grizzly. "He was right here," she told them as their three horses stopped to graze on the tender green grass. "I was so scared my heart was thumping." She paused and looked around the quiet meadow. "It was only a week ago. It seems like forever."

"I had a talk with your dad about bears." Alison shuddered. "He gave me the lowdown on grizzlies. Basically, they'll stay out of our way if we're careful to stay out of theirs."

"And we should stick together and make lots of noise so they hear us coming," Meg added.

Becky nodded. She didn't have to worry about coming up to the mountain alone anymore. At least for this summer there would always be the three of them. "A week ago, I thought I'd die if I had to stay here." She shook her head. "It's amazing what a difference friends make."

"Your mother said we might even see a wild mustang up here some day," Meg went on. "She said they used to roam all over this range. Wouldn't *that* be amazing?"

Alison gazed down at the ranch buildings. "What about Henry?" she asked. "What's going to happen to him?"

"Well, Mr. Douglas fired him when he found out he wasn't a groom," Becky said. "Henry doesn't know what he's going to do. He might still try to get to California, or ..."

"He might ask your dad for a job on the ranch." Meg grinned. "I think he likes the cowboy life."

"He's just a fancy fake cowboy," Alison sighed. "I prefer the real thing."

Meg and Becky grinned at each other. It was going to be an interesting summer!

About the Author

As a kid, Sharon Siamon was horse crazy. How crazy? She never walked—she galloped everywhere on an imaginary horse. At school, she organized a whole gang of riders, who headed for the ranch in the corner of the school yard every recess and lunch hour to play horses. At home she lured the huge workhorses on her neighbor's farm over to the fence with apples, then clambered on their backs and rode like the wind until they scraped her off under a low-hanging hawthorn tree. She grew up, still wishing for a horse, and taking every chance she got to get near horses, read about horses and ride them. She's been writing horse books ever since for kids who love to dream about having a horse of their own.

Sharon is the author of many books including eight Sleepover Series titles and a number of Stage School Series titles under the pseudonym Geena Dare. The Mustang Mountain Series has already been translated into German, Finnish, Norwegian and Swedish.

More Mustang Mountain Titles

#2: Fire Horse (1-55285-457-4)
Meg, Becky and Alison go in search of two horses missing from the ranch, only to find the animals have joined a band of wild mustangs. When a forest fire rages through the mountains, the girls must find a way to bring the horses back to safety.

#3: Night Horse (1-55285-363-2)
Mustang Mountain's favorite mare is about to foal, and the sire is a wild mustang with a bounty on his head. The mysterious young men around the ranch might intrigue her friends but Becky suspects one of them might be the bounty hunter.

#4: Wild Horse (1-55285-413-2)
Alison doesn't want anything to do with horses. Her horse has been sold and she has to spend her holiday in a cramped cabin in the middle of nowhere. But Becky and Meg have a chance to see real wild horses, and they're not about to let Alison's bad mood ruin it.

#5: Rodeo Horse (1-55285-467-1)
Becky and Alison are introduced to the fast-paced world of barrel racing by Sara and her beautiful palomino. They're headed for the biggest rodeo of them all — the Calgary Stampede — when an accident derails their plans. But was it an accident?

#6: Spirit Horse
The legend of a mighty black stallion haunts the Mustang Mountain trails. When Meg, Alison and Becky test their horses against the worst the wilderness can throw at them, they call on the spirit of the great horse to help them.